"Aren't you curious?"

"Curious about what?" she asked.

"What a kiss would be like."

She looked up into those wicked green eyes and knew curiosity spelled danger. "Why would I be curious?" she asked, wishing her voice didn't sound so shaky.

"Because you're a woman, and women are curious." He hooked a finger under her chin. "Just as I'm a curious male."

"Cameron—" His name came out a rasp, the sound barely audible over the thudding of her heart. "We shouldn't. You said it yourself. Things could get complicated."

"No, this is to keep things from getting complicated. This is a way of diffusing the pressure."

WHAT ARE *LOVESWEPT* ROMANCES?

They are stories of true romance and touching emotion. We believe those two very important ingredients are constants in our highly sensual and very believable stories in the LOVE-SWEPT line. Our goal is to give you, the reader, stories of consistently high quality that may sometimes make you laugh, sometimes make you cry, but are always fresh and creative and contain many delightful surprises within their pages.

Most romance fans read an enormous number of books. Those they truly love, they keep. Others may be traded with friends and soon forgotten. We hope that each LOVESWEPT romance will be a treasure—a "keeper." We will always try to publish

**LOVE STORIES YOU'LL NEVER FORGET
BY AUTHORS YOU'LL ALWAYS REMEMBER**

The Editors

AMERICAN BACHELORS:

THRILL OF THE CHASE

MARIS SOULE

BANTAM BOOKS

NEW YORK · TORONTO · LONDON · SYDNEY · AUCKLAND

THRILL OF THE CHASE
A Bantam Book / December 1995

If you would be interested in receiving protective vinyl covers for your
Loveswept books, please write to this address for information:

Loveswept
Bantam Books
P.O. Box 985
Hicksville, NY 11802

ISBN 0-553-44504-9

Published simultaneously in the United States and Canada

ONE

"Meet me at four-thirty," he'd said.

Peggi Barnett glanced at her watch and shook her head. It was now five-thirty and still no Cameron Slater. For a man who'd been so adamant about needing his condo refurbished *immediately*, he certainly wasn't very punctual.

Not that she'd stood around for the last hour twiddling her thumbs and aimlessly waiting. She'd come to look over his condominium, and that was exactly what she'd been doing. The doorman had let her in, and notebook, pencil, and measuring tape in hand, she'd checked out every room, from the foyer to the terrace, all three thousand square feet, taking measurements and jotting down ideas.

She'd gotten lots of ideas . . . especially in his bedroom.

There was something about mirrors over a man's bed that quirked her imagination. Of course, it didn't help that just last month she'd seen Cameron Slater's name and picture in an article about Chicago's most eligible bachelors. The reporter had described him as a devilishly handsome rogue, sexy, and not at all what the reporter had expected.

Peggi could understand the journalist's reaction. That morning had been her first meeting with Cameron Slater, and to look up from a swatch of fabric and see an Adonis dressed in an Armani suit coming toward her wasn't what she'd expected either.

It hadn't been easy keeping up a facade of cool, calm efficiency, not with her heart racing a mile a minute and her temperature soaring. If she'd passed him on the street, she'd never have pinpointed him as a financial consultant. He simply didn't fit the image. Even wearing a suit, his muscular build was evident. The cut and style of his golden-brown hair was just too long and unruly for a businessman, the gleam in his green eyes too wicked. He better fit her image of a football player or an actor.

One very sexy football player or actor.

Peggi shook her head at her thoughts and tossed the turquoise-and-salmon throw pillow she'd picked up back onto his sofa. What Cameron Slater looked like didn't matter, nor did her reaction to him. He'd come to her because he was looking for an interior designer, nothing more.

She had welcomed him into the shop and had rearranged her schedule to meet with him that afternoon because she needed his business. So where was he?

Waiting always irked her, and she had half a mind to leave, to walk out, scribbling a message about what he could do with the job.

She smiled at the idea, then laughed. As if she would.

They were talking about a lot of money here, and

not about just *one* job. All interior designers depended on word-of-mouth advertising and recommendations to build their businesses. If Cameron Slater was satisfied with her work, he would recommend PDQ Interiors to others, and from what she'd heard and read, he gave financial advice to some of Chicago's richest and most influential people. Getting his endorsement would make up for the damage she and her big mouth had done back in April. No longer would she and Darlene be struggling to make ends meet and wondering if they'd made a mistake in opening their own business. No longer—

Her beeper went off, jerking her from her dreams of money and success back to reality. Darlene wanted her to call, and Peggi could guess why.

Slater had phoned and canceled.

She used the telephone in his kitchen, and Darlene answered on the second ring. Peggi cut her off before she finished saying, "PDQ Interiors."

"It's me, Dar."

"Oh, good." Darlene's voice lost its formal tone. "Are you finished with Slater?"

"I haven't even gotten started. I thought that's why you were calling. So far he's a no-show."

"Where are you, then?"

"In his condo. The doorman let me in. My instructions were to look around until he arrives." Peggi glanced at the atrocious wallpaper in the kitchen. "You ought to see this place, Dar. He wasn't kidding when he said the decor was tacky."

"That bad?"

"Terrible. It's like a bunkhouse set for a grade-B western."

"How long are you going to wait for him?"

Peggi checked her watch again. "I don't know. I have a few more measurements to take. If he's not here by the time I'm finished, I'll leave."

"Is there a radio there?"

The question puzzled Peggi. Stepping to the kitchen door, she could see a radio in the living room. It was part of a huge entertainment center. "Yes."

"Well, while you're taking those measurements there's a new talk show you should listen to. It's called *Austin in the Evening*, and they're running this segment called 'Fiona's Forum' that you should call in to."

"*I* should call in?"

"Uh-huh. Fiona—Fiona Alexander—is a psychic who claims she can find a soul mate for men who can't commit. Maybe she can find one for Craig."

"Craig can—"

Darlene cut her off. "I know—'rot in hell.' Okay, maybe this psychic can find a soul mate for you."

That, Peggi thought, would be something new. So far, every man she'd fallen for had either turned tail and run the moment he sensed their relationship was getting serious, or had flatly stated that marriage wasn't for him.

"The number's 919-555-7792," Darlene went on. "Give the station a call. What can you lose?"

"This job, when Mr. Slater finds out I used his phone to call a talk show long distance so I could find a mate. And what's this psychic going to do, give me a name and number to call?"

"She hasn't done that so far, but she has given a couple of the callers general descriptions of what their soul mates will look like. She's also talked to a physics professor who's looking for psychics, and even warned one caller that the man she was calling about had better watch out because the woman he's destined to fall in love with is holding a gun."

"A gun?" Peggi wasn't sure she'd heard that right.

"That's what she said. Fiona's talking to a real winner now." Darlene chuckled. "Just before they broke for commercials, this guy called marriage a confining, inhibiting institution that drains the life out of people. You really should turn it on just to hear him. He'll make your blood boil."

Peggi wasn't sure she needed her blood boiling; nevertheless, after hanging up, she walked into Cameron Slater's living room and turned on the radio. As far as she was concerned, if Slater objected to her listening to a talk show, tough. A woman forced to rearrange her schedule, then wait for over an hour, deserved a little entertainment.

It took her a few seconds to find the station Darlene had said the talk show was on, but when she heard, "We're back with *Austin in the Evening*," she knew she had it.

"If you just tuned in, folks," the talk-show host said, his voice reminding Peggi of a circus barker, "this portion of the show is called 'Fiona's Forum,' and I have the talented psychic Fiona Alexander in the studio with me. Before the break, we were talking to John. You still out there, John?"

"I'm still out here," another man answered, his voice deep and gravelly and strangely familiar.

"John?" a woman broke in, nothing familiar about her voice. Peggi assumed it was the psychic, Fiona. "Are you sure you want me to call you John?"

There was a moment's pause before the caller answered. Even then, his yes was hesitant.

The way he said the word piqued Peggi's curiosity.

Forgetting the measuring she still had to do, she sat on the edge of Cameron Slater's massive turquoise-and-salmon striped sofa.

"Before the break," Fiona said, "you called marriage an inhibiting institution, said it was confining."

"It is," John answered firmly. "Get married, and what happens? You lose your freedom, your personality, and your ability to think for yourself. Marriage is not a partnership, as all the love brokers would have you believe, but a parasitic relationship. It sucks the strength out of both parties."

"You've never been married, have you?" Fiona said, more a statement than a question.

"You don't have to jump into a fire to know you're going to get burned. I have eyes. I have ears. I know what I saw while I was growing up, what I hear in the locker room, on the golf course . . . everywhere I go. My married friends all envy me."

"Oh, give me a break," Peggi muttered. "Envy you what?" She liked the sound of his voice, its rough tone oddly arousing, but she didn't like his attitude. From what he'd said, she doubted that he needed to worry about losing his freedom or personality. No one would want him, and she questioned if he had a personality to lose.

"You should not be afraid of marriage," Fiona responded calmly.

"I'm not afraid."

"Right," Peggi disagreed. She'd heard that before, and then the guy took off.

"Statistics show married men are happier than single men," Fiona continued.

"Statistics can lie."

Yes, Peggi knew his type. No matter what you told

them, they wouldn't believe you. This caller had made up his mind, and no one was going to change it.

Fiona tried. "How are you going to feel when you're in your fifties and sixties and all alone?"

"If I have my health, I'll feel great. And who's to say I'll be alone?" He chuckled. "I just won't be married."

"Just like . . ." Fiona's voice trailed off, then she made a side comment. "Very interesting, Austin. We have two for one here."

"Two?" the talk-show host asked, obviously confused.

Peggi didn't understand either.

Fiona came back strong and clear. "I now understand the significance of what you're saying, but I hope you know, sometimes what seems to be is only what we want to see."

"I'm not going to argue with that," John said. "It's exactly what I've been saying. Many a marriage seems to be great, but once you look below the surface, you discover things are different."

"Every marriage has its problems, but once you meet the right woman—"

"Right woman?" John interrupted. He laughed, the rumble deep and throaty. "I can't begin to tell you how many women have tried to convince me they were the *right* woman for me."

"But they weren't," Fiona agreed.

"They were just fools," Peggi said, and sighed. "Like me." But she was through being a fool, through trying to be the "right" woman for guys who didn't want to get married.

"Don't give up yet," Fiona said softly, and Peggi stared at the radio. It was eerie, but for a moment she would have sworn the woman was speaking personally to her.

John brought her back to reality. "Look, Fiona," he said seriously. "You say you can match men up with their soul mates. But what if a man doesn't want to be matched up? What if he has everything he wants without this soul mate?"

"And do you have everything?" Fiona challenged. "Is John happy?"

"Very happy," John insisted. "No one is depending on me; I'm not tied down."

Fiona chuckled. "You think you have everything under control, don't you?"

"Not everything. But what I can control, I do."

"Like the way you stop seeing a woman if you begin feeling anything for her?" Fiona asked.

"How—" John began, then stopped himself. "It's just better that way."

Peggi shook her head at John's answer. Boy, oh boy, this guy was Craig all over. "I could fall in love with you," he'd said the last time she saw him.

She'd suspected that night that he wasn't pleased with the realization, and she'd been right. He never called again. One more Mr. Right who'd turned out to be Mr. Wrong.

Again, Fiona chuckled. "Things are going to change. And soon. John will welcome this change with open arms."

"That's what you think," he argued.

"That's what I know," Fiona said firmly. "As for you—"

He interrupted again. "Nothing's going to change my mind. I've seen what love and marriage can do to people and I want no part of it. You can set me up with a woman, but I'm not going to marry her. I can assure you, I'm never getting married."

"Bully for you," Peggi grumbled, and snapped off the radio. She didn't need to waste her time listening to another man giving reasons why he didn't want to get married. What she would like to hear for a change was a man giving reasons why he *wanted* to get married.

Giving reasons to her.

The next guy who wanted to date her was going to get asked the marriage question right away. Was he for it or against it? If he said he wasn't interested in marriage, then *c'est la vie* and good-bye. No more false hopes. No more heartbreaks.

Walking over to the living-room window, she stared out at Cameron Slater's expansive view of Lake Michigan. From twelve stories high she could see across the seemingly never-ending expanse of blue-gray water and look down at Lakeshore Park and the Navy Pier. A tour boat hugged the shoreline, its deck lined with tourists. Another two months and the sight-seeing boats would be idle. Three months from now Cameron Slater wanted this job finished. It was time to get her mind off men and marriage and back to business.

Peggi picked up her notebook and measuring tape.

When she'd talked to him that morning, he'd said he'd never been pleased with what his last decorator had done, but that he hadn't made any changes for personal reasons. She'd wondered then what to expect, but she hadn't been prepared for what had met her eyes when the doorman had let her in.

A Southwestern decor did not fit this high-rise, nor did it match the personality of the man she'd met that morning. Tacky was an understatement. The only things missing were a black velvet painting and a branding iron. The three terra-cotta pots in the corner were gross, the primitive stone table in front of the couch laughable. In her opinion, his last decorator should have been shot.

She heard a key in the front door and sucked in a breath. Quickly she brushed her hair back from her face, then adjusted her glasses on the bridge of her nose.

Cameron Slater, it seemed, had arrived.

Finally.

Cameron knew she was still inside. At least, the doorman had said he hadn't seen her leave. Being an hour and fifteen minutes late was not a good way to start a working relationship, but he did have an excuse—at least for one hour of that time. The last fifteen minutes had been spent foolishly.

He saw her the moment he entered his living room. She stood by the center window, the smile on her face warm and welcoming. "Ms. Barnett," he said, switching his briefcase to his left side and extending his right hand as he walked toward her. "So sorry to have kept you waiting."

Her handshake was firm, but the quirk of an eyebrow let him know he would need the excuse. "I'm afraid," he said, having practiced his speech on the elevator ride up, "that I was unavoidably detained. One of my clients, a woman in her eighties, had a stroke last month. She's doing much better, but it's difficult for her to talk, and I couldn't just leave. We had some papers that had to be gone over. Did you look around?"

"I did."

"And?"

A smile danced in her brown eyes, and she freed her hand from his. "You're right. This place does need an overhaul."

He'd known that from the day he'd returned from his travels and seen the finished product. Hal had been so proud. Cameron could still remember his old buddy's expression as he showed off each room.

There was no way Cameron could tell Hal that day that he hated it. And there was no way he could tell him later, because within a month the unattractive, overstuffed furnishings had become a memorial.

For two years Cameron had lived with mirrors over his bed, chairs with wagon wheels for sides, and stone-topped tables. But the cow's skull had gone out immediately, along with the spurs, the velvet painting, and the branding iron. Now he wanted everything else out, and before Christmas.

"Overhaul to your heart's content," he said. "But I want final approval on everything you do."

"I would expect that." She looked around. "It's not going to be cheap."

"I'm sure it won't be." On the other hand, he was also sure her quote would be lower than some interior designers around Chicago. He'd done his homework. Peggi Barnett and Darlene Lawrence had established PDQ Interiors just a little over two years ago. Like most new businesses, they were struggling to find a niche in the market. Peggi was the interior designer; Darlene created customized window treatments and bed coverings. Everyone he'd talked to had said Darlene was a whiz with a sewing machine and Peggi was an outspoken dynamo who wore wild clothes and had an eye for good design.

Her eyes, at the moment, were focused on his face, a frown furrowing her brow. "Is there a problem?" he asked.

"I don't know." She tilted her head slightly. "Your voice . . . It sounds like . . ." She glanced toward his stereo system, then shook her head and smiled at him. "Just a coincidence, I'm sure."

He liked her smile.

He liked the entire package.

The glasses she wore didn't lessen the impact of her expressive brown eyes, and she had a gorgeous mane of honey-blond hair, a knockout face, and a body to go with it. She was tall, maybe five-eight or nine, and curved in all the right places. She also knew how to dress to catch the eye. The people he'd talked to were right about the clothes. There was no ignoring the blue tights and blue suede boots or the multicolored smock top that came to just below her hips.

There was no ignoring the tightening in his loins, either, though that was exactly what he planned to do.

She might be single and currently not involved with anyone—he'd discovered that while checking out her business—but he wasn't interested. One thing he'd learned in his thirty-four years was that it wasn't a good idea to date anyone he was doing business with. Things could get uncomfortable.

And so could the next few minutes.

"You're not going to like what I have to say," he began.

Her smile disappeared. "Which is?"

"That besides making you wait for over an hour,

I'm now going to have to back out of this appointment."

The frown returned. "Back out?"

"I thought I'd be here by four-thirty and that we'd be done by five-thirty. It's nearly six now, and I have a dinner meeting at seven. Could we possibly meet tomorrow morning?"

She shook her head. "I can't tomorrow. My nephew's having his tonsils out at ten, and I promised to be at the hospital with him." She looked around the room. "Perhaps tomorrow afternoon?"

Damn! He could kick himself for missing this meeting. Tomorrow afternoon was out. He was booked solid. He shook his head.

"The next time I have open is Friday," she said. "At eleven."

"Friday morning at eleven," he repeated, and pulled a daily planner from his briefcase. He had a luncheon date with Mitch, but that could be canceled. He'd tell Mitch when he saw him. Which would be in—

Cameron glanced at his watch.

Mitchel Delaney was supposed to pick him up in exactly five minutes.

Cameron snapped his daily planner closed and dropped it back into his briefcase. "Friday at eleven it is. Now, if you'll excuse me, I've got about five minutes to take a shower and change."

"Of course."

She turned and walked across the room to where a large leather purse sat on the floor. He watched her lean over to pick it up. The hem of her multicolored top rose higher on her body, and he caught a clear view of her blue-covered bottom.

The tightening in his loins became almost painful. When she straightened, her hair falling back around her shoulders like waves of honey, he quickly turned away and started for his bedroom, afraid his body might betray his thoughts. "See you Friday," he repeated.

"You'll be here?" she asked. "At eleven?"

He glanced back, grinning. "I promise to be standing at the door when you arrive. I want to get this started right away."

"I took some measurements and made a sketch of the floor plan while I was waiting for you. I just need a few more measurements." She glanced toward his living-room windows. "I could get them before I leave, then it would probably only take me an hour or so to finish this initial consultation."

"Go ahead." He waved a hand toward his living room. "Be my guest."

Peggi waited until Cameron's bedroom door closed behind him before she loosed a sigh of relief. Good Lord, what was she letting herself in for? The guy oozed sex appeal from the top of his golden-brown hair to the tippy toes of his leather shoes. How could she do any work for him when simply looking into his eyes had her heart revved up like a Formula 1 racing car?

This was crazy. She didn't normally react to men this way. Sure, she admired a good-looking man. What healthy, all-American woman didn't? But to actually have her legs go rubbery?

No, that wasn't like her.

What she needed to do was ignore him, forget that he made Tom Cruise, John Kennedy, Jr., and Mel Gibson all look like wimps. He was a job, that was all. Or at least she hoped he would be a job. Until he signed a contract, nothing was for certain, and if she didn't come up with some ideas he liked, he would take his business elsewhere.

Setting her purse back down, she walked to the window and started taking the measurements she needed. Heights and widths were jotted down in her notebook, electrical outlets noted, as well as built-in light fixtures and the placement of their openings. Back at her drafting table she would convert the numbers and notes to floor plans and sketches.

As she worked she heard his shower come on and tried not to think of him standing naked under the water. She'd only seen him fully dressed, yet she could imagine what his arms would look like without a jacket and shirt covering them, how those biceps would glisten when wet, and how his chest would be covered with golden-brown hairs that would catch the water and guide it into rivulets that would slide down over his flat belly to his—

Peggi shook off the thought.

Business, she told herself. She had to keep her mind on business.

The water went off, and she unconsciously sighed again and tried to hurry. She didn't want to be around when he came out. All she needed was one more measurement.

A knock on his front door caused her to drop her measuring tape. The metal casing hit the windowsill with a clatter, then fell to the carpeting.

"Can you get that?" Cameron yelled through his bedroom door. "It'll be Mitch."

"Sure." Her hand shaking, she left the tape on the floor and headed for the door.

"About time," the man in the hallway said the moment she opened the door, then he stopped, his gaze dropping from her face to slowly travel lower. He was smiling when he looked back up. "Well, hello. I know you're not Cameron and you're definitely not his housekeeper."

She grinned and held out her hand. "I'm Peggi Barnett, his potential interior designer, and if you're Mitch, Mr. Slater will be out in a minute."

"Peggi." Mitch held on to her hand as he walked into the condo and closer. "I swear, Cam finds the best-looking women in Chicago."

"Well, thank you." She slipped her hand free and stepped farther back into the room. "I was just getting some measurements." She glanced down at the pencil and notebook she held, then back toward the window where she'd left her measuring tape. "One minute and I'll be out of here."

"Don't rush because of me," Mitch said, still smiling.

"That you, Mitch?" Cameron asked from behind Peggi, and a shiver ran down her spine. Strange as it might be, Cameron Slater's gravelly voice did sound just like the caller's on the radio. Slowly, she turned to face him.

He stood in the doorway to his bedroom, dark trousers hugging his hips and legs, but no shoes or socks on his feet and no shirt covering his muscular arms and tanned chest.

The mat of golden-brown hairs she'd imagined only minutes earlier glistened with tiny droplets of water while a few slid seductively down over a taut belly toward an unbuckled belt. She felt a tightening in her own stomach and knew the response was foolish. It didn't matter that there wasn't an ounce of fat on his body or that his biceps were molded with a sculptor's finesse. It didn't matter that she'd never been so aroused by the sight of a half-naked man. He was a potential client, nothing more, and staring at him like a starving woman looking at a feast was ridiculous.

She pulled her gaze away.

"I thought I was late," Mitch said, "but it looks like you're running even later." His smile took on a knowing edge when he glanced her way. "But I can understand why."

Peggi knew Mitch had the wrong idea if he thought something was going on between Cameron Slater and her. "I—" she began, but Cameron interrupted.

"I stood her up, too, Mitch. Mitchel Delaney meet Peggi Barnett, my new interior decorator."

Peggi smiled. No need to explain that she was a designer, not a decorator.

"You do decorate an interior," Mitch said, then he glanced around the room. "Glad to see you're finally going to do something about this, Cam."

"I figured it was time. You about done?" he asked her.

Peggi nodded. "I just need to get my tape."

"Don't chase her off," Mitch said, grinning suggestively. "We were just getting to know each other."

Cameron turned to go back into his bedroom. "Behave yourself," he said, his chuckle deep and rumbling. "I'll be just a couple more minutes."

His laugh even reminded Peggi of the man on the radio show. She knew it was crazy, but still she couldn't stop herself from calling after him. "Mr. Slater, do you sometimes go by the name John?"

"You heard it too," Mitch said, glancing her way. He turned toward the bedroom, where Cameron had gone. "You won't believe what replaced our five o'clock stock report. A talk show with a psychic. I was listening on the way over. One of the callers, a guy who identified himself as John, sounded just like you, Cam."

"Should have," Cameron said, coming back out of his bedroom, buttoning a white dress shirt. "It *was* me."

TWO

"You?" Peggi stared at Cameron. "But . . ."

"Car phone," he explained. "I heard that woman telling the world she could name a person's soul mate, and it irked me. The way she was talking, you'd think marriage was the epitome of all that was good, and a man who didn't want to get married was just some lost soul who needed her guidance."

"So you called and gave her a false name?" Peggi found that less than noble.

"I didn't think it a good idea to use my real name. Up until tonight, there was a stock report on at that time. Some of my clients might have been listening. Besides, it wasn't exactly a false name. John is my uncle's name, and he shares my opinion."

"That marriage stinks?" She'd picked up that much from what he'd said on the radio.

"I should have known it was you," Mitch said, and laughed. "So what did you think of Fiona's prediction?"

Cameron glanced his way. "Which one? The

woman couldn't make up her mind. One minute she's telling me my soul mate will be contacting me in the very near future; the next, she's saying my soul mate is waiting for me. I couldn't believe it. What a phony."

"A charlatan," Mitch agreed in full camaraderie.

The laughter they shared irked Peggi. "You talk about charlatans? You're the one who gave her a false name. You—"

Both men ceased laughing and looked at her. It was Cameron who spoke. "What's so terrible about using an alias? Writers do it all the time. Besides, she's supposed to be the psychic. She should have known."

"How could she—" Peggi stopped herself and grinned. "She did know. That's why she asked if you were sure you wanted her to call you John, why she told that talk-show host they had two for one."

The self-assured smile left Cameron's face, replaced by a frown. "She was playing a role, making general statements, that's all. You don't really believe some woman at a radio station in North Carolina could tell who was calling, do you? I mean, that's as naive as believing she could ask a few questions and come up with the perfect mate for a man."

"Say what you like," Peggi said. She wasn't sure what she did believe about the woman's psychic powers, but she disliked Cameron's implication that she was naive. "It sure sounds as though she knew you were talking for two people. That's why she said John would welcome the change with open arms." Peggi remembered more. "Why, she said, 'As for you—'"

Mitch picked up on the idea. "She did mention two. One who would be in contact, and the other who would be waiting." He grinned at Cameron. "Waiting for you."

Cameron glared at his friend and grumbled something. Peggi wished Mitch had kept quiet. The idea that she might be Cameron Slater's soul mate was too ludicrous even to consider. Quickly, she switched from that point. "The whole reason for that show is to get people talking, get men and women to realize that just because one relationship didn't work doesn't mean another won't. People need hope, need to keep looking for the right person."

"Assuming there is a 'right' person or that marriage is a beneficial state." Shaking his head, Cameron walked toward her. "You want to know what the real idea is behind that program, Ms. Barnett? It's to hook listeners like you, women who are sure that happiness is just a matter of finding 'Mr. Right.' Women who need someone to look after them. You listen, the ratings go up, advertisers buy more time, and the station makes money."

Seeing him half-dressed across the room had turned Peggi's stomach upside down and sparked her imagination. Watching him come closer, the scent of his freshly showered body subtly playing with her senses, she couldn't stop the tremble that skittered through her. She forced herself to keep her gaze on his face.

"Are you sure, Mr. Slater?" she asked tensely. "I think the purpose of that program is to hook listeners like yourself. You're the one who called in, not me. In fact, I turned the program off before you'd finished making a fool of yourself."

Mitch chuckled. "I guess she told you."

Cameron ignored him. "Are you saying that if a man doesn't want to get married, he's a fool?"

"I'm saying a man who thinks he's God's gift to

women is a fool." Purposefully she let her gaze drop down his body.

The golden-brown hairs covering his chest were curlier than she'd realized and looked soft to the touch. She followed their trail as they tapered downward until her gaze reached the point where his shirt came together. Beneath the crisp white material was a slight bulge. The end of his unbuckled belt, she was sure, but the image still triggered her imagination. She forced herself to bring her head back up slowly, and though her heart was racing, she managed to keep her expression controlled. Nevertheless, the mocking glint in his eyes said he knew she wasn't as calm and cool as she was pretending.

"I never said I was God's gift to women."

"But you did say," she reminded him, distressed that her voice sounded a bit breathless, "and I quote, 'Who's to say I'll be alone? I just won't be married.'"

"So?"

He didn't understand, and his smug smile fanned her irritation. "I'm surprised you don't have notches on your headboard. Are the mirrors above your bed so you can admire yourself?"

"You've been in my bedroom?"

"I was told to look around while waiting for you. I did."

"The mirrors were not my idea."

"Right." She let her smile relay her disbelief. "I suppose you were forced to put them there."

"No, but I—" He stopped himself, frowning. "Look, what I have in my bedroom is my business. Whether I want to get married or not is my business too."

"Not when you broadcast it across the country on

the radio. I'm sick of hearing you men give reasons why marriage is so terrible. Let me tell you, marriage can be beautiful—a fulfilling and happy experience. Believe me, I know. I've seen marriages like that."

"And I've seen—"

She interrupted. "I know, 'Marriages that are inhibiting and confining.' Boy, do I know your type."

"And what type is that?"

Icicles could have hung from his words. She didn't pay any attention. She was on a roll. "You see what you want to see, even that psychic mentioned that. You use the bad as an excuse, as a reason not to commit. Marriage is a partnership, a give-and-take situation. You don't know how to give, only how to take."

His expression didn't change, but she noticed the green of his eyes was darker and his nostrils were flared. "Are you finished?" he asked, his voice low and tense.

"Yes," she said, then changed her mind. "No. As far as I'm concerned, anyone who has to control his feelings has real problems. I feel sorry for you, Mr. Slater."

"Well, don't. The one with problems seems to be you."

His facade of calm was gone, and she sensed the storm about to erupt, but his words goaded her on. "And why do you say that?"

"From what I've heard, you and your partner aren't exactly experts on successful relationships. Didn't her husband run out on her? And how old are you? Twenty-seven? Twenty-eight? How many boyfriends have you had?"

"None of your business," she said defensively.

"Didn't you tell Myra Gibson you were a loser when it came to serious relationships?"

Peggi stared at him. She'd said that to Myra in confidence. Or so she'd thought. It seemed her love life was now being broadcast throughout Chicago.

Cameron smiled. "I did a little checking on you and your partner."

"Snooping sounds more like it."

"They say you're outspoken. Some find it an endearing trait. Others find it annoying enough to warrant firing you."

"That's only happened once," Peggi said.

"Looks like it's happened twice."

"Twice?" she asked, then understood. A sickening lump hit her gut, but she kept her voice steady. "You can't fire me."

"Oh?" His eyebrows rose in question. "And why not?"

"Because I haven't accepted the job." Picking up her purse, she straightened and looked him in the eyes. "I can let myself out."

"Glad to hear that," he said coolly.

Head held high and her chin forward, she walked toward the door. Mitch stepped back but didn't say a word.

After the door closed behind her, Cameron shook his head and resumed buttoning his shirt. "Guess that takes care of that."

"Guess it does." Mitch laughed. "If she's the one the psychic was talking about, you're in for rough ride."

"I'm not taking any rides, and I don't believe in psychics."

"Whatever you say. But Peggi was right; the woman was pretty psychic to know you weren't John."

"If she did."

"Why else would she say John would be hearing from the woman he loved and your woman was waiting for you?"

Why indeed? Cameron wondered, the question bothering him.

He loosened his slacks and tucked in his shirt. "I'll believe in psychics the day my uncle tells me the woman he loves has contacted him." He chuckled at the possibility. "Come on, Mitch. You know my uncle John, you've heard his thoughts on marriage. From the time I was nine and he came back from his world travels, I've heard him brag about how he's avoided the trap. He's not trading his freedom to coddle a woman and he won't let some woman jerk him around. If Uncle John is in love with someone, it's going to be news to him."

"Think he heard that program?" Mitch asked.

"I doubt it." Cameron pulled up his zipper with a flourish. "Would you or I have heard it if they hadn't taken the market report off and replaced it with that show?"

"I can't believe they took the market report off."

"My exact sentiments."

Mitch chuckled. "I also can't believe you called in."

Cameron found it difficult to believe himself. "It was the way they were going on about finding the right woman for every man that got to me. They were making not getting married sound like a disease."

Mitch nodded toward the closed door. "*She* made it sound like a disease."

Cameron snorted, also looking at the door. "She's another one of these women who thinks marriage will solve all of her problems. And one of these days she probably will find some sucker willing to take care of her, but it's not going to be me."

"You could do worse. She sure had a nice pair of—" Mitch grinned —"legs."

"Legs"— Cameron also grinned "—aren't everything. As outspoken as she is, a guy would be bailing her out of trouble all the time. I don't need that."

"Might be interesting."

"Playing the market is interesting. Trying new restaurants is interesting." He shook his head. "Getting involved with a woman with marriage on the brain is trouble."

Mitch looked around the room. "So what are you going to do about redecorating this place?"

"Find someone else to do it. I have a couple other names on my list."

Cameron stared at his front window, then looked down at the floor as a circular silver object caught his attention. He walked over to check it out.

"You going to have everything done by Christmas?" Mitch asked.

"Before Christmas." Cameron leaned down and picked up the tape measure.

Peggi drove directly back to the shop. The bell above the front door rang wildly when she stepped inside, and Darlene came out from the back, a length of fabric and a needle and thread in her hands. As petite as a pixie and looking very much like one, she frowned when she saw Peggi. "What's wrong?"

"I blew it again." Peggi dropped her purse on the counter by the cash register and ran her fingers through her hair, giving it a punishing pull. "When will I learn to keep my big mouth shut?"

"What happened?" There was no accusation in the question.

Peggi shook her head. "I told him what I thought of him."

"You told him he turned you on?"

"No." Peggi had forgotten her conversation earlier that day with Darlene. Peggi's comments about the attraction she felt had been uttered before she knew Mr. Cameron Slater's opinion of love and marriage. "I told him he was self-centered."

"Because he was late?"

"No, because he was the caller on that talk show. He was John."

"John? I thought his name was Cameron."

"It is. He used his uncle's name."

"But why?"

"He said he didn't want his clients knowing he was the caller."

"And you told him what you thought about men who won't marry?"

Peggi nodded. "And lost the job."

Instead of getting angry, Darlene laughed. "I wish I could have been there."

"So do I." Peggi closed her eyes, remembering the way Cameron had looked standing in the doorway of his bedroom. Seeing him half-naked hadn't been nearly as earthshaking as when he'd walked toward her, that shirt of his half-open, exposing his chest and titillating her imagination. Looking up into his eyes and feeling so overwhelmed by his nearness was one memory she wouldn't easily forget. Even now the thought sent shivers through her. She shook off the sensation and opened her eyes.

"If you had been there," she said, "maybe you could have muzzled me."

"Maybe, maybe not." Darlene grinned impishly. "But it would have been interesting to see his reaction after what the psychic said."

"What did the psychic say exactly? I couldn't stomach listening to him and turned off the program before he was finished."

"So you didn't hear? Well, it was confusing, but now I understand. She said John would soon be contacted by the woman he loved. Then—and this was the confusing part at the time—she said, 'And the woman for you is waiting.' And there you were, waiting."

"Because the guy made me wait. I'll tell you one thing for sure, I am not the woman for Cameron Slater."

"But you do find him attractive. I haven't forgotten what you said this morning."

"*Did* find him attractive," Peggi corrected her. "Before I knew his views on marriage. He's just like Craig. Any woman who falls for him is going to end up with a broken heart."

"This is going to be interesting."

"What's going to be interesting?"

"Seeing what happens."

"Nothing's going to happen. That's the problem. I was fired. We hadn't even gotten into the consultation, and I was fired. I won't be seeing Mr. Cameron Slater again, won't be getting the job or the fee, and won't be getting any recommendations from him. I'm really sorry, Dar."

"So forget it," Darlene said nonchalantly. "Who

knows. Tomorrow an even better job might come along."

"That I'll probably blow because of my big mouth. Sure you don't want to get another partner?"

"Never." Darlene wrinkled her nose and smiled. "You're the best. It's the people who don't want to hear the truth who are the losers."

Peggi appreciated her friend's support, but *they* were going to be the losers if she didn't start using more tact. Best or not, bills had to be paid. "You know what's really depressing?"

"No, what?"

"I would have loved doing his place." She looked around their shop. "Not just because of the money the job would have brought in, but because his place was gorgeous . . . or it could be. You would have loved his windows."

"Good shapes?" Darlene asked.

"Pretty standard, but the views out of them are fantastic. His living room and bedroom face Lake Michigan. The other bedrooms, one of which he's converted into an office, face downtown."

"What's he have covering them now?"

Peggi shook her head. "Drapes. Heavy, dark things. He refers to the guy who did his place as a decorator. It definitely wasn't an interior designer . . . wasn't anyone who has any sense of light and design."

She could have done so much with his place, made it a showcase of her talents. If she'd just kept her mouth shut.

But she hadn't.

❧━━━━━❧

They were ten minutes into their drive to dinner when Mitch chuckled. Cameron glanced his way. "What's so funny?"

"I was just thinking it was a good thing Pat wasn't waiting for you when you got home tonight."

Since his housekeeper usually left around one in the afternoon, Cameron was sure he was missing something. "Why was it a good thing Pat wasn't there?"

"Can you imagine yourself married to her?" Again, Mitch chuckled.

"I can't imagine myself married to anyone." And certainly not to his housekeeper. The woman was a middle-aged taskmaster. "What brought that on, anyway?"

"I was still thinking about that talk show. What a coincidence that that psychic tells you there will be a woman waiting for you and one is there."

"No coincidence at all," Cameron insisted. "I'd gone to PDQ Interiors this morning and set up the meeting. In fact, if I hadn't been delayed at Mrs. Weimer's, Peggi Barnett would not have been waiting but would have arrived a half hour after I got back."

"*If,*" Mitch said, exaggerating the word. "That's the key. *If* you hadn't set up the appointment, and *if* you hadn't been delayed, and *if* you hadn't turned on the radio to hear the stock report, and *if* it hadn't been replaced by a talk show, and *if* you hadn't called in to that show . . ."

"And *if* I believed in that garbage," Cameron said, hoping to end Mitch's bizarre reasoning.

"Don't you find it strange that a psychic a thousand plus miles away knows someone will be waiting for you?"

"Strange? No. A good guess? Yes. A playing of the odds."

"She sure didn't like what you had to say about marriage."

"The psychic?"

"No, your interior decorator."

"Ex–interior decorator," Cameron reminded him. "And she calls herself an interior designer."

"Wasn't it just yesterday that you told me this PDQ Interiors was exactly what you wanted?"

"That was before tonight."

"She got to you, didn't she?"

Cameron glared at him. "What's that supposed to mean?"

"She's quite a looker."

"I've known better."

"You afraid of her?"

"Of course not."

Mitch laughed, and the sound grated on Cameron's nerves. "Now what?"

"She's quite outspoken."

"Quite."

"An interior decorator—excuse me—interior designer and a financial consultant. What a pair."

Cameron scowled out the side window. "There's not going to be any pairing."

For a few minutes Mitch said nothing, and Cameron tried to wipe the memory of his run-in with Peggi Barnett from his thoughts. He had more important matters to consider. In approximately ten minutes he would be sitting down to dinner with a group of men and women who expected him to know what direction the market would be going in the next few months and what companies would be the best investments. No easy task considering no one ever truly knew what the market was going to do, but he did pride himself on the fact that his predictions had been better than most in the last three years . . . except in one case.

That "one case" was the problem.

"You still going to get your place redecorated?" Mitch asked. It was the one question that needed to be faced.

Cameron didn't see a choice. "I have to. Because of that damn company going belly-up, I lost that bet. Which means this year I have to put on the Christmas party for the Investment Club members. I am not putting on a party for twenty of the richest men in Chicago and their wives with my place looking as it does now."

"You could always reserve a suite at the Hilton."

"I could, but I'm not going to if I can help it." Tradition was that the loser always hosted the Christmas party at his home. It was expected.

"What are these other two decorators like that you have on your list?"

"Cummings recommended one; Haynes the other. What more can I say?"

Once he'd made up his mind to plunge into the mess of redecorating, Cameron had gotten a list of interior designers from friends and business associates. The two best known designers everyone assured him would do a fabulous job were so booked that it would be a year before they could take on his place. The next name on his list was a man one of his flakier clients had recommended. Cameron had talked to the man less than ten minutes, and he knew he wasn't about to let the guy touch his place. It would have been Hal all over.

After that, he did a little checking, which eliminated more names, and by the time he got to Peggi Barnett and PDQ Interiors, he was wondering if he would ever find a decorator. When she said she could do the job in the allotted time, he was ready to hire her on the spot.

"What's the PDQ stand for?" Mitch asked.

"She said the *P* stood for Peggi and the *D* for Darlene, and they just added the *Q* to give it a catchy sound. The *Q* could stand for quality or quick." He needed both.

"I'd use her if I were you."

"After what she said?"

"So the woman thinks you're self-centered and disagrees with you about marriage. She's entitled to her opinion. Since when did you start surrounding yourself with yes-men . . . or should I say 'yes-persons'?"

They both knew how he felt about that. In frustration, Cameron grumbled, "Since this evening, evidently. I don't know. Considering how she feels, I doubt she would work for me."

"She'll work for you." Mitch glanced at him and grinned. "Use a little of your charm."

THREE

Peggi recognized Cameron the moment he stepped out of the elevator, all dressed in his business suit, his hair slightly disheveled. For a moment she thought their being at the hospital at the same time was merely an unlucky coincidence, then his gaze met hers, and he smiled and started toward her.

Suddenly she felt sick, a giddy sensation coiling in her stomach. A reaction to the hospital aromas and no breakfast that morning, she hoped. She certainly didn't want to think seeing Cameron Slater could bring on this response.

He was the enemy. She'd proclaimed that loud and clear to her sister only a short time ago, and to Cameron personally yesterday evening. Dammit all, he'd teased her with a job that could have turned their business around, had dangled it in front of her like a golden carrot, then he'd fired her.

She should hate him, or be indifferent at best. Instead, here she was, having to remind herself to breathe and hoping, as he neared, that he didn't notice the flush of color rushing to her cheeks.

Why did he have to be so damned good-looking? Why couldn't he have been thin and anemic or short and fat, have a wart on his nose or a high-pitched whiny voice? Why couldn't he be the one wearing glasses right now? Thick, ugly glasses with tape holding them together.

No. Cameron Slater had to be the image of physical perfection—tall, handsome, and if not dark, at least nicely tanned.

Her gaze dropped to his chest. Their encounter the evening before had eliminated the need to imagine the muscling beneath his suit jacket and crisp white shirt. She'd seen the sinewy arms and broad chest, knew how the hairs curled and swirled beneath the starched cotton. He not only defied her image of a financial consultant, he teased her needs as a woman, which was exactly what upset her.

Don't even think of liking him, she reprimanded herself. He's not interested in marriage.

The thought helped. She took in another breath and coolly asked, "What brings you here?"

His steps slowed a bit, his eyebrows lifting quizzically, but he kept smiling. "I dropped by your shop to see you. Your partner reminded me that you were here. How's your nephew?"

"Joel's fine. The operation was a success, his tonsils are out, and my sister's with him in the recovery room right now." A side trip to the bathroom was the only reason Peggi wasn't also with Dana and Joel. She wasn't sure if she should bless her small bladder or curse it. "What did you want to see me about?"

Cameron had been prepared for a frosty reception,

but he was facing a stone wall. Nothing in her rigid posture and clipped words gave him encouragement. He reached into the right pocket of his slacks. "You left this at my place last night."

She looked at the measuring tape he held toward her, a frown crossing her brow, then she cautiously took the metal casing from his hand. "Thank you for returning it." Her gaze returned to his face. The wide circles of her glasses gave her an owlish appearance, and the message in her brown eyes was one of wariness.

"I could have left it at your shop," he said, knowing she didn't believe he'd tracked her down just to return a measuring tape. "But I wanted to talk to you about last night."

Immediately she was defensive. "What about last night?"

"It's clear we have different views of marriage."

Her laugh was short and sarcastic. "Quite different."

"Considering I'd made you wait for more than an hour then rescheduled our appointment, you were probably a bit upset with me."

"A bit." Her parroting his words was giving him no hint to how receptive she might be to his proposal. *Use your charm*, Mitch had said. If the two calls he'd made that morning had been more encouraging, he wouldn't have to use his charm.

Since they hadn't been encouraging, he smiled warmly and kept his voice soft. "You know, considering the short time you and your partner have been in business, you have a very good reputation."

"We try to please the people we work with," she said smoothly. "But, as you pointed out last night, I'm outspoken, brash, and a real loser."

"That's not exactly what I said."

"Pretty darn close, I'd say. So why are you here?"

"To see when you can start working on my place."

That stopped her for a moment, her eyebrows lifting and a flash of surprise streaking through her eyes. Just as quickly, she covered her reaction. "And what if I don't want to work on your place?"

"That's your decision, of course. And the job won't be easy, not with the timetable I'm imposing. But I do think you would find it worth your while."

That was all he would offer. He would not cajole. He would not beg. Mitch might have convinced him that he'd been hasty in his actions last night, but he wasn't groveling. Maybe she was the only interior designer on his list who had the time to get his place ready before Christmas, but that didn't mean she was his only choice. He hadn't tapped into the general listing of interior designers around Chicago. There had to be a number of them within a fifty-mile radius who could do as good a job or better than Peggi Barnett. One, certainly, should have time for him.

"Why the change of heart from last night?" she asked.

He could understand the question and the suspicion in her voice. She was no fool and would have him jumping through a hoop if she guessed how desperately he needed her. He worded his answer carefully. "I believe we got off on the wrong foot. What I want is my condominium redecorated. We're talking a business arrangement. Personal opinions about love and marriage —yours or mine—shouldn't enter into this."

"I'm not into designing playboy penthouses."

"I'm not looking for a playboy penthouse."

"And I won't do something slipshod just to meet your deadline."

"I don't want anything slipshod. I entertain clients at my place, men and women who trust my judgment to manage their money. Subjecting them to a Southwestern look has been bad enough. I'm not going to make a change for the worse."

She frowned. "Why did you let your original decorator do something you didn't want?"

"Misguided loyalties," Cameron admitted. "Hal was a friend . . . a friend who had fallen on hard times. When he went into the decorating business, I thought giving him the job of decorating my place would be the boost he needed. I also thought he understood what I wanted. It wasn't until I got back—"

Peggi shook her head, interrupting him. "You didn't know what he planned on doing?"

"He gave me a general idea. It sounded fine."

She shook her head again. "How much experience did this guy have?"

"A little." Cameron wasn't about to admit he'd been Hal's first client. He probably didn't have to. She'd seen his place. "I'll be around this time."

"Breathing down my neck?"

The moment she said it, Peggi wished she hadn't. Cameron's glance toward her neck was brief, but long enough to send a tremor of anticipation down her spine. She needed to clarify her position.

"If I accept this job, you'll know exactly what I plan on doing before I even start. If something I suggest doesn't suit you, it will be changed."

"Unless my name is Jeanne Smith-Bova?"

She grimaced, the experience of working with

Jeanne Smith-Bova still making her cringe. "There is a limit to the number of changes a designer will make."

"I don't know her personally," Cameron said. "But others I talked to said they didn't blame you for telling her what you thought of her changing her mind every other day."

"She may have had money and time to waste, but I didn't."

"From what I heard, you lost money on tht job." He smiled. "Doing my place could offset that loss, and a good recommendation from me . . ."

He let the sentence hang, but she understood. "Or a bad one?" She could imagine he'd be a nasty foe. "What happened to Hal's business after he did your place?"

"Hal died a month after he finished my place," Cameron said solemnly, and looked down the hallway. "Right in this hospital."

He cared about this Hal, Peggi realized. That was why he'd left his condominium as it was even though he disliked it. He might not believe in marriage, but he did believe in loyalty.

"Get my place done by the first of December," he said, "and there will be a bonus."

He was pushing all the right buttons, and she had a feeling he knew it. As much checking around as he'd done, he probably knew to the penny the financial position of PDQ Interiors and how much they needed his money. She also had a feeling she should tell him to go to hell and take his business with him. Working side by side with him was not going to be easy.

If she'd been the only one involved, she might have done just that—told him to take his job and shove it—but she wasn't alone in this. Darlene's money was also involved, money she'd inherited from her grandmother. Dar had had enough hard knocks—the death of a baby and a husband running out on her. Emotionally, as well as financially, she needed the business to succeed, and that couldn't be ignored.

"I still can't see you until Friday at eleven," Peggi said, willing to give in to financial necessities but wanting some leverage.

"Friday at eleven it is." He held out his hand. "At my place."

Looking him straight in the eye, Peggi shook his hand and prayed she wasn't making a mistake.

Although it wasn't Friday the thirteenth, as far as Cameron was concerned, it might as well have been. From the moment he'd gotten out of bed, things had gone wrong. First he'd knocked his alarm clock off the nightstand, cracking the plastic casing, then Pat had called, saying she was sick and wouldn't be coming to work much less staying late to cook for guests. He had a messy house, no one to clean or cook, and dinner guests arriving at six. Worst of all, by ten o'clock the Dow had dropped fifty points thanks to the triple witching, an occasional Friday phenomenon in the market that always resulted in hectic, nerve-racking trading. He was definitely feeling bearish when the doorman rang at eleven. "What?" Cameron growled into the intercom.

"A Ms. Peggi Barnett is here to see you," the man answered formally.

"Send her up."

Cameron glanced at his watch. Allowing two hours with Peggi, he should be in good shape. He could run a vacuum himself and catch any dust that had dared sneak in since Pat's last onslaught with the dust rag. The Millers' plane was due in at O'Hare at three-thirty, they'd be checking into their hotel sometime after four, and should arrive at his place around six. After drinks and his excuses, he would take them to one of the nearby restaurants. They liked the Chop House. All he had to hope was that the stock averages were up by the time the market closed or George Miller would be in a stew. As many times as Cameron had assured the man that his portfolio was well diversified, whenever the market dropped, he went into a tizzy. Hand-holding was a big part of being a financial consultant.

Feeling confident that everything was under control, Cameron waited at his open door for Peggi to arrive. The moment she stepped out of the elevator, he knew control was a matter of perspective. Seeing her sashay down the hallway, dramatically dressed in a white suit with big black buttons, the fringed hem of the skirt barely making it midway down her thigh, he certainly couldn't control the tension that surged through his body or the direction his thoughts headed.

It was lust, he knew, pure and simple. The male libido kicking in and heightening his blood pressure. It was also an unwanted feeling. Peggi looked at life through rose-colored glasses, was the marrying kind. They were as opposite as day and night.

"You're here," she said, her tone implying she hadn't expected him to be.

"I said I would be." Of course he'd also said that the last time.

"I brought a few sample books for you to look at."

It was then that he noticed the portfolio she carried under her right arm. Oversized and thick, it might have caused a shorter person some problems, but she barely seemed aware of its bulk. It did, however, pull her suit jacket tight across her chest, emphasizing the fullness of her breasts. He forced himself not to stare, focusing on her eyes instead.

"No glasses?" he asked.

"I'm wearing my contacts." She shook her head, her hair falling in soft waves over her shoulders and enticing his gaze lower again. "The infection's gone."

"Infection?" He breathed deeply as she passed him and entered his condo. Her perfume was light, not completely masking the enticing feminine smell of her body.

"Eye infection," she explained, stopping in the middle of his foyer and looking around. "Where do you want to work?"

The bedroom flashed through his mind, an image of her naked on his bed and showing him room designs. He vanquished the idea with a blink of his eyes and looked toward his dining area. The massive wood table Hal had insisted was all the rage was a much safer location. "There okay?"

"Fine."

She was all business, going directly to the table and laying her portfolio on top. He closed his front door, but didn't immediately go to her side. Standing back, he watched her spread drawings and samples over the tabletop. She leaned forward, stretching the white linen of her skirt tight across her bottom, and Cameron decided Peggi Barnett had an absolutely delightful behind. He also decided the thoughts racing through his head were crazy. He didn't want an affair with this woman, and even if he did, she didn't want anything to do with him. She'd made that quite clear the other night. To make a move on her would be as insane as putting all of his clients' money in derivatives and would end basically the same way—he'd be the loser. He'd obviously been spending too many nights at the gym or working at the computer. The way he was reacting, he needed the company of a woman, a woman who *wasn't* looking for commitment or love.

Straightening, Peggi gave the display a final look, then pushed her hair back from her face and glanced his way. "I think I'm ready."

So was he, Cameron told himself. No more crazy thoughts. From now on his mind would be focused on furniture styles and color schemes. Satisfied with his decision, he walked toward her. Yet he couldn't help grinning. If Peggi Barnett had any idea how few times he'd been with a woman in the last six months, she'd certainly change her view of him as a playboy. It was almost funny.

Almost.

"So what do you think I should do with this place?" he asked, stopping beside her and looking down at the sketches she'd made. To his surprise, they weren't design ideas but simply floor plans showing the wall space, openings, and outlets, and giving dimensions.

She smiled. "I think you should keep it."

"What I mean is, how should it be decorated?"

"That's what we're going to decide today . . . or at least we're going to start the decision-making process."

"I want everything done in three months," he reminded her.

"Don't worry." She patted the back of his hand, the gesture quick and casual yet surprising him. She reached for one of the catalogs she'd placed on the table. "We'll make your deadline. What I need to find out now is what you like and don't like."

What he liked was easy. He liked having money, mingling with people who had money, and being his own boss. What he didn't like was the surge of excitement that had shot through him at her touch. Disturbed, he studied her, not the catalog she'd opened.

Peggi could feel his gaze on her and cursed herself for touching his hand. Being a "toucher" had its drawbacks. Most people didn't mind, actually seemed to like the contact, but there were always a few who drew back, erecting a wall, and those who took it the wrong way. Though Cameron hadn't actually drawn back, she sensed a tension in him, and she wasn't sure how he'd taken it.

"First of all," she said, attempting to ignore his penetrating gaze and hoping he didn't think she was trying to start anything, "I need to know what you like in furniture styles. Modern? Traditional? Antiques?"

"I like what looks good," he said, still staring at her.

She glanced at him. "And what looks good to you?"

For a moment his gaze seemed to encompass her and she thought he was going to smile, then he glanced around the room, a frown drawing his brows together. "Not what's in this place." He finally looked down at the book she had open on the table. "Or that."

He'd pointed at a room arrangement displaying Queen Anne–style furniture. It was a start. She turned the page. "What about these?"

He studied the two room layouts depicted, then pointed at the more contemporary of the two. "That's nice."

Again she turned the page. "And these?"

Once again, he preferred the more contemporary of

the two. As she turned the page again the telephone rang. He hesitated, then stepped back. "I'd better get it."

Peggi breathed a sigh of relief when he walked away. Before she'd left the shop that morning, she'd made up her mind how she was going to handle this job. She would be herself, no kowtowing simply because she needed his money to solve her and Darlene's financial problems. If he didn't bring up what he'd said on that radio show, she wouldn't either. Their different philosophies of life should have nothing to do with the job. She would deal with him as a client and ignore him as a man.

The only problem was, ignoring him wasn't going to be easy. Standing close to him, she'd been all too aware of him. His scent was clean and masculine; his voice, with that gravelly intonation, both soothing and arousing. She watched him pick up the phone in the kitchen, his muscles bunching beneath the cotton of his long-sleeved shirt, and could remember how he'd looked without a shirt on, could imagine how it would feel to have his arms wrapped around her.

Quickly, she glanced back at the sketches and catalogs she'd laid out on the table. He's not interested in marriage, she told herself. You're only going to think of him as a client.

"Why hi, Edna," she heard him say into the phone, his tone warming as he spoke. "What a surprise to hear from you. Oh, you're in already. So are we still on for six?"

A date. Peggi kept staring at the catalog. She should have guessed.

"Well, I thought we'd have a drink here, then go out for dinner."

Right, she thought. They'd have a drink, maybe two, but Peggi doubted they'd get much farther than his bedroom with the mirrors on the ceiling.

"Oh, really?" Cameron hesitated. "I'm sorry to hear that."

Peggi mocked a sad face from where she stood, certain he couldn't see.

"No, no problem," he assured the Edna on the other end of the line. "Of course I still want you to come."

Of course, Peggi repeated to herself, and turned back to face him, wondering how long it would take him to convince this Edna not to cancel their date.

"What is it George can't eat?" Cameron picked up a pencil and began writing on a notepad by the telephone. "But he can have pasta and beans." He nodded and jotted down more notes. "No milk. Olive oil is all right, you say? No, it won't be any inconvenience. Yes, I'm sure he's worried about the market. Tell him not to. It's just one of those Fridays. Everything should be back to normal by Monday. Yes, I know how he is. See the two of you at six, then?"

Peggi wasn't sure what she thought now, and Cameron's expression when he set down the receiver stated loud and clear that he had a problem. He looked her way. "I'm sorry. I've got to make a call before we go on."

"No problem," she answered, and watched him pull out the phone book. Under the circumstances, she didn't feel there was much more she could say. Besides, he would be charged for this time. How he wanted to spend it was up to him.

When he made his first call, she truly began to understand the situation. She assumed it was a restaurant he dialed. He explained he had out-of-town guests coming and that one was on a restricted diet. When he asked what the restaurant served that would fit that diet, she gathered the answer was "nothing."

He made three other similar calls, then looked in a new section of the Yellow Pages. This time the way he explained the situation to the person on the other end of the line, Peggi knew he was trying catering services.

The results were the same.

Ten minutes later he slammed down the phone and stared at the cupboards in front of him. She saw him take in a deep breath, his chest expanding beneath his shirt, and saw him flex his shoulders before he looked at her. His expression was apologetic. "Just a couple more minutes," he promised, and walked by her and into his office. He pushed the door closed.

Now come the girlfriends, Peggi thought. She could imagine what he would say when he called. *Honey, can you help me?* Grinning, she pulled out a chair and sat down.

The clock in his living room kept ticking, and she amused herself by flipping through the catalogs and sample books she'd brought and marking certain pages she thought might have items he would like. Half an hour later the door to his office opened and he stepped out. He wasn't smiling. She rose to her feet and waited for him to approach.

"Do you cook?" he asked.

"Me?"

"Yes. Could you whip together a dinner that didn't use any milk, sugar, or meat and only a minimal amount of certain oils?" He wrinkled his nose. "And make it not only look good but taste good?"

"I take it you couldn't find anyone to come in and cook for you?"

"The caterers I called either said they were booked for tonight or they didn't do special diets on such short notice. And"—he paused, glancing back toward his office—"the other calls I made didn't pan out."

"Tsk-tsk." She grinned. "I guess I overestimated your influence with the women."

"Evidently." He frowned at her. "This isn't funny. George Miller is an important client, and at six o'clock tonight he and his wife will be at that door"—he pointed at his outside door—"expecting to be fed." Once again, he shrugged, his anger dissipating. "I'd throw something together if I knew what to fix."

"My partner collects cookbooks. I'm sure she has some for special diets."

"Can she also cook?"

Peggi laughed at the idea. "Trust me, you don't want her cooking."

"But you think she would have some recipes?"

"I can give her a call and find out."

"I'd bless you." He smiled. "Come up with something I can throw together, and I'll cross your palm with silver."

The mortgage payment on their shop was due, and though Darlene had some money in the bank, it was all that was left from her inheritance, and they'd agreed to save it for a rainy day. "Cross my palm with lots of silver, and *I'll* cook your dinner for you."

Cameron held out his hand. "It's a deal."

FOUR

"You're now going to cook for him?" Darlene asked when Peggi returned to the shop.

"It's not a volunteer thing. He's paying."

"I don't know." Darlene's blue eyes twinkled. "You're making me wonder. One day you're telling me you'll never work for the man, the next you're saying you are, and now you're cooking for him."

"Just this one time," Peggi insisted, dropping her portfolio in her office before following Darlene through the shop.

PDQ Interiors was housed in a two-story brownstone. In the 1950s, the living room, dining room, and parlor had been separated from the other rooms and converted first into a craft shop, then a dress boutique, then a used-book store. All of them had ultimately failed.

Two years ago Darlene and Peggi had bought the property with a low down payment, a lot of glib talking, and a thirty-year mortgage. There were days when

Peggi considered the purchase a blessing; other days when she wondered if they'd been out of their minds.

As an interior-design shop, the setup was ideal. The neighborhood already had several small shops that attracted women, and since women usually initiated changes in decor, it was natural for them to stop by an "interiors" shop to get ideas.

They would step into a small foyer decorated with a working fountain, a dramatic stone statue, and a painting Peggi had done her first year in college before switching her major to interior design. The fountain and statue were too heavy to steal, and she kept hoping some street punk would snatch the painting.

To the left of the foyer, the parlor was used for presentations, as the library for their samples, and as her office and work area, with her drafting table near a window. To the right of the foyer, the original living room was filled with items for sale, everything from colorful throw pillows to tea towels. Their cash register was located there, and a TV and VCR that ran continuous tapes on decorating tips. The old dining room was off the living room, its walls covered with paintings sold on consignment, its floor space crammed with unique items Peggi and Darlene had found at auctions and estate sales, bought at a bargain and sold for a nice profit. In addition, each window in the three rooms was used to display a different window treatment.

Darlene lived in the remaining rooms of the house, an arrangement that both solved her housing problem and cut down on the number of employees needed to run the business. She could be in the kitchen, or upstairs in her bedroom or sewing room, and the ringing of the bell over the door would alert her that someone had entered the shop.

No one was in the shop when the two of them stepped into the kitchen.

"I can think of three cookbooks that might work," Darlene said, kneeling to go through the stacks piled in a cupboard under the counter. "How fancy do you want to get?"

"Not very. I have to have this ready by six o'clock tonight."

"Is he going to help?"

"I hope so." Peggi squatted beside her, taking the books Darlene pulled out. Considering Darlene's cooking talents, which were close to nil, her vast collection of cookbooks always amazed Peggi, but she'd gotten used to Darlene coming back from estate sales with not only items for the shop but also more cookbooks to add to her collection.

"I know this one has a lot of recipes that don't use fat, milk, red meats, or refined sugars," Darlene said, handing her the third book. "Have you changed your mind about him?"

"Not at all." There wasn't anything to change. "I just see this as a sure way of paying this month's mortgage payment."

"He doesn't make your heart race a little?"

"No," Peggi lied.

Together they pored over the books, Peggi marking recipes that sounded good. The shop bell rang twice and Darlene went out to the help the customer while Peggi continued reading. It was one o'clock by the time she had a menu and shopping list.

"Want me to come along and help?" Darlene asked.

Peggi knew her timing was going to be close. She also knew having Darlene in the kitchen wouldn't help.

"No, I'll be fine," she said. "Mr. Playboy can chop and peel. It's his party, after all."

Peggi repeated that sentence when the doorman let her into Cameron's condo. "It's his party, and he's not even here."

"He said he'd be back as soon as he could," the doorman answered, carrying the two grocery sacks he'd taken from her into the kitchen. "If you need anything, you're to call him at his office."

"If I need anything," she mumbled after the doorman had left. "I need my head examined, that's what I need."

Frustrated, she glanced around the kitchen. She'd been appalled the first time she saw the knotty-pine cupboard doors with the CS brand in the center of each. Once you added the wallpaper with the branding-iron motif, tacky didn't begin to describe the decor.

The architect, on the other hand, had designed a very efficient kitchen. Everything had a place, and everything was in its place. Finding that "place" was her problem.

She opened cupboard doors and drawers, pulling out pots and pans, spoons and spatulas as she discovered them. Soon the counter was covered with utensils and she began the chopping and peeling, blanching and sautéing. Every so often she checked the clock on the stove. Time was passing too quickly. There were too many things to do.

Cameron walked through his front door at four o'clock. All the way back from his office, he'd cursed the news media. One article on dropping oil prices, and Ted Moss had wanted out of all commodities. What an afternoon to have to completely revamp a man's portfolio. Cameron had wondered if he would ever get Ted out of his office.

The musky, woodsy aroma of frying mushrooms and the pungent smell of garlic greeted him. Cameron heard a spoon clink against a bowl, and once he stepped into his dining area, he could see Peggi, her honey-blond hair pulled back from her face and held at the nape of her neck with a black scarf. An apron covered the front of her white suit, and she'd abandoned her heels and stood in her stocking feet, a run angling its way up her left leg.

She studied the book propped open in front of her, stirring with one hand and adding ingredients with another. Her actions had a hurried air, yet there was a grace to her movements. He watched, aroused by the pure femininity of her, and for a moment wondered if she'd be as graceful in bed.

But just for a moment.

Clearing his throat, he walked into the kitchen. "Sorry I had to leave. This has just been one of those days."

She glanced his way, neither smiling nor frowning. "Do you have any sea salt?"

"Sea salt?"

"That's what the recipe calls for." She shrugged, her small sigh poignant. "I guess I'll have to use regular salt. Cross your fingers."

He didn't like the sound of that. "You sure you know what you're doing?"

She did frown then, storm clouds sweeping across her eyes, and he knew he should have kept his mouth shut. Stepping back from the counter, she held the wooden spoon she'd been using toward him. "You want to take over, you're more than welcome."

"No." He'd learned from his mother that the kitchen was a woman's domain. "You're the boss."

Her expression softened. "Meaning if anything goes wrong, it's my fault. Right?"

He hadn't thought of it that way, but he supposed she was right.

Not waiting for an answer, she turned back to the recipe book. "These are definitely different ingredients from what I usually use. Thank goodness for health-food stores. I just never thought about salt."

Salt was salt, as far as he was concerned. Going over to the stove, Cameron lifted the lid of the pot in front. Inside was a yellow mush.

"Polenta," she said before he asked. "Basically cornmeal mush."

"So what's the menu?"

"Tempeh-stuffed mushrooms and a tofu dip with fresh vegetables for appetizers. A cucumber-cilantro salad, then polenta with mushrooms, asparagus with a Chinese black-bean sauce, and stuffed rainbow trout with tofu sauce. For dessert, apple crisp."

"The apple crisp sounds good." He wasn't sure about the rest with all the tofu and strange-sounding ingredients. Steak and potatoes were his usual fare, especially the steak and potatoes at the Chop House. If Edna hadn't called and said George was on a special diet, that's where they would be eating that night.

If. The word was beginning to bug him. He looked at Peggi. "What can I do to help?"

She glanced toward the dining room. "Could you set the table and bring me whatever serving dishes you use?"

He slipped out of his suit jacket, loosened his tie, and rolled up his sleeves, then quickly set the table, putting out four of everything. When he was sure all was ready, he called her into the room.

She nodded when she saw the table, then walked over to a place setting. "Close."

He watched her switch the positions of the spoons and forks, set a third fork above the plate, and move a water glass to the right.

"But not close enough?" he asked, altering the place setting in front of him.

She looked up at him, the width of the trestle table separating them. Her grin said it all.

"I never could get it right," he admitted.

"Few men do." She straightened a napkin, then gave the table a sweeping look. Seemingly satisfied, she headed back into the kitchen.

He followed. "You've helped a lot of men set tables?"

At the counter near the stove, she stopped and glanced back. "I thought you knew all about me."

"Not all that much, really." Only enough to know she picked losers, men who loved her and left.

"Just what Myra Gibson told you?"

He nodded, seeing no reason to lie. "She really liked you—said you were honest, dependable, and very talented. She loves what you did to her house."

"She was easy to work with," Peggi said, remembering the three months she'd spent on the Gibson house and the delightful conversations she'd had with Myra. They'd talked about everything, including men. Peggi hadn't expected the woman to repeat those conversations to someone like Cameron Slater.

She glanced up at him. "In the future, I'll have to remember to watch what I say to clients."

"It wasn't pure gossip. When I asked about you, she

warned me not to mess with you, said you'd been hurt enough times by men like me. I assured her that I make it a policy not to get involved with anyone I work with."

Peggi caught the message. "The control bit again?"

He frowned. "I consider it good business sense."

"You're probably right." She wasn't going to argue. If that psychic on the talk show hadn't gotten anywhere with him, why should she think she could? Picking up a knife, she began mincing an onion.

"I know I'm right," he said. "If you get involved with someone you work with, things can get complicated . . . too complicated."

"Could get downright messy." But then, life could be messy. "Also, it's hard for a man to run away from someone he has to work with."

"I don't run away."

She didn't miss a chop with her knife. "No, not at all."

"I don't," he insisted, then changed his tack. "Look, I thought we agreed not to let our different opinions regarding love and marriage enter into our working relationship."

She looked up from the onion. "I didn't bring up the subject, you did. I have no intention of getting involved with you. In fact, an affair with you is the last thing I would want."

"Is that so?" He huffed and turned away. "Well, for your information, not all women share your feelings."

She watched him walk to the refrigerator. "Are you bragging or complaining?"

"Neither." He glanced back at her. "Just stating a fact."

"Opinion," she corrected him.

"Whatever," he muttered, and looked into the refrigerator. Peggi grinned and went back to mincing the onion.

He was upset, and perversely, that pleased her. The man was too damned cocksure of himself, too certain women found him absolutely irresistible.

Too bad he was right.

His voice alone, with its deep, rough intonation, was enticing. Add the body and those beautiful green eyes . . . Cameron Slater was one lethal man. She just had to make certain she didn't become one of his victims.

She heard the refrigerator door close and the hiss of a bottle cap opening. She was curious, but she didn't look his way, not until he spoke. "Want a beer?"

He held a dark bottle, his posture relaxed. He was in control again, the man in charge. She shook her head.

"Need any help?"

She glanced at the containers and raw ingredients she'd placed on the counter. "Sure."

"What can I do?" He walked over to her, and she knew what he could do. He could stop wearing whatever aftershave or cologne he had on. It made him smell too good. And he could stop breathing. The sound, so near to her ear, made her heart race.

From the side of the chopping block, she grabbed a plastic bag and handed it to him. "I bought fresh asparagus. It needs to be washed and trimmed."

"You had enough money for everything?"

He'd given her cash and orders to make sure she bought the best. She had. "It was more than enough. I'll give you your change later. I take it these people are important clients?"

"Very." He stepped to the sink and began rinsing the asparagus. "I don't know how long George has been on the *Forbes* 400 list, but he was a multimillionaire long before I began handling his accounts at Chicago Fidelity. When I told him I was going to start my own business as a financial consultant, he went with me. Being able to mention his name as a client made a big difference in my success."

She glanced his way. "I read an article about you. It said most of your clients are millionaires, and if they aren't when they start with you, you see to it that they become so."

His smile was sly. "Sounded good, didn't it? You always want to give the impression that you're the best."

"It wasn't true?"

He shrugged, then turned back to the asparagus. "I work with some very wealthy people. I also work with some who are happy to end up with a tidy little nest egg to retire on."

"I could use a nest egg." Peggi lightly coated the bottom of a large skillet with olive oil and placed it on the stove. "I tell people I'm now earning in the six figures. What I don't tell them is four are in front of the decimal point and two are after it."

Cameron chuckled and watched her sauté the onion she'd minced along with crushed garlic. She added just a dash of salt, then minced mushroom stems and basil. It all looked delicious until she opened a jar and crumbled some of its contents into the skillet. "What is that?" he asked, not sure he wanted to know.

"That's the tempeh." She turned off the fire under the pan, gave the mixture a stir, then lifted the jar and read the label. "It's cooked, fermented soybeans."

It sounded terrible. "You sure this is going to taste good?"

"Trust me," she said, a teasing glint dancing in her eyes.

How often he'd heard that before, but tonight he really had little choice. "George isn't a man who likes change, or at least he didn't. Since he moved down to Georgia . . ."

Peggi spooned the mixture she'd created into mushroom caps. "I don't know what else to fix." She glanced at the clock on the stove. "And it's getting late."

Very late, he realized. "What else do you need done?" The asparagus was clean, the ends all snapped off. "These are ready."

She looked at her list, then shook her head. "Most everything else I have to do. It's just a matter of mixing and cooking."

"Then I'll be in my office. I should do some paperwork before George and Edna arrive."

In the bedroom he'd converted to an office, Cameron pulled out George Miller's file and placed it on his desk. A flick of his thumb and he had his computer on. Two minutes later he was logged into the closing market report.

From the kitchen, he heard the buzzer on the stove go off. A second later it was quieted. From what he'd seen, Peggi had everything under control.

You think you have everything under control, don't you? That's what the psychic on that talk show had said. He stared at his monitor. Did he?

Or was he as big a fool as his father? Was he once again being manipulated by a woman?

He didn't seem to be able to control the reactions

of his body when Peggi Barnett was around. Or the thoughts that kept slipping into his head. Why he'd even wondered what she would be like in bed was beyond him. But he had wondered . . . did wonder.

Myra Gibson had warned him to leave Peggi alone, and he had every intention of heeding her advice. He'd been without a woman for too long, that was all. What he was feeling was lust. Problem was, in this day and age, a man didn't just pick up a woman to satisfy his needs. It was too damned dangerous. And developing a relationship led to problems. He'd learned that well enough.

Peggi had asked him if he was bragging when he'd said other women wanted to get involved with him. In a way, maybe he had been, maybe he'd wanted her to know that even if she didn't want him, others did.

"Why even care?" he muttered.

"You always talk to your computer?"

The sound of Peggi's voice so near to his chair startled him. He jerked his gaze away from the monitor and looked up at her. She stood only inches away, a bowl in one hand, a carrot in the other. Her stockinged feet had made no sound on the carpeting.

"Would you mind trying this vegetable dip?" she asked. "Something's missing, but I'm not sure what."

She dipped the end of the carrot into the mixture and held it toward him. He reached out, taking her hand in his and guiding the carrot toward his mouth. Her skin was soft and warm, his fingertips picking up the rapid beat of her pulse.

Even as he bit into the carrot, letting the dip roll over his tongue, he watched her eyes, seeing the flicker of awareness in them. She could say she wasn't interested, but her body was telling him a different story, the color in her cheeks a sign that she wasn't as cool and calm as she was pretending.

Slowly, he chewed, letting the tip of his tongue slip out and slide over his lips. The taste of the dip was unusual; the woman before him intriguing.

Her eyes darkened, turning a cocoa brown—steamy and sweet—and then she laughed, the sound enticingly sensual. "You make eating a carrot look sinful," she said.

"You ought to see me eat an apple," he said softly.

"Eve wouldn't stand a chance." She pulled her hand away from his touch. "What do you think?"

He thought a roll in a bed with her would ease a lot of the strain in his body, and probably the strain in hers, and that he was insane even to entertain such an idea. "I think it needs more salt."

She nodded and stepped back. "I'll give it a try."

The kitchen was warm, but Peggi knew the temperature had nothing to do with the heat of her skin. She loosened the top two buttons of her jacket and fanned herself. Never again would she bite into a carrot without thinking of how Cameron had looked when he took a bite. His eyes had spoken volumes, all of it terribly tempting. Maybe he'd said he didn't want a relationship, but that wasn't the message she was getting.

"Forget it!" she muttered, and shook salt into the dip. Twice burned should be often enough to develop a thick skin.

No more putting herself in a position where she could get hurt. No more listening to her hormones. Chemistry be damned! She would ignore him and his sexy body, his wicked green eyes, and that tantalizing cologne. She could do it.

She would do it!

Again, she shook salt into the dip.

At five-thirty, Peggi softly knocked on the doorjam of Cameron's office. He glanced up from the sheet of paper he'd been studying. "Everything is as ready as I can get it," she said. "If you've got a minute, I'll show you what needs to be done just before you're ready to eat."

"Show me?"

"If I cook the fish before I leave, it will be all dried out when you go to eat it."

"Why are you leaving?" He stood, flexing his arms and shoulders, the ripple of muscles beneath his white shirt drawing her gaze like a magnet. "You're not afraid to eat this food you've been preparing, are you?"

"Of course not. But when I saw the other place setting—" She'd assumed he'd found a date and that woman would finish up what she'd started.

"It's for you," he said. "I figured you'd stay. Not just to cook, but to keep Edna company. I know she'd like to have another woman around."

"I don't know." Peggi hadn't considered the possibility.

"Do you have another date? A pressing appointment?"

She could say yes, probably should. On the other hand, the fish needed to be closely timed, the sauces heated to just the right temperature, and if Cameron got talking business, the meal she'd just spent hours preparing could be ruined. "Do I look all right the way I'm dressed?"

His gaze skimmed her from head to toes, his expression giving no hint to his opinion. Reaching forward, he caught the ends of the black silk scarf she'd used to tie her hair back. Slowly, he slid it off, watching her, and she held her breath, aware of how close his arms were to her face and how the golden-brown hairs on his forearms curled ever so slightly.

A smile touched his lips when he combed his fingers through her hair, spreading it across her shoulders. His knuckles brushed her cheek, and she heard her own intake of breath.

"You look fine," he said softly, his caressing gaze touching her lips.

And then the scarf was in her hand, and he'd turned away. "You can use the bathroom down the hall to freshen up."

George and Edna Miller were in their sixties. Dapper was how Peggi would classify George, his top hat, glasses, and gold-handled cane all adding to the image. He looked like a man who had money—lots of it—and she had a feeling he liked people knowing it.

Edna was his showpiece, a fur coat draped over her shoulders and lots of diamonds hanging from her earlobes, around her neck, and on her fingers. She might have been a beautiful woman once, but now her features were pinched and her forehead seemed frozen in a scowl.

"George, Edna," Cameron said. "I'd like you to meet Peggi Barnett, my interior designer and your cook for the evening."

George shook her hand. Edna merely smiled and asked, "Have you done any homes I would be aware of?"

"She did Myra Gibson's," Cameron answered, taking Edna's coat.

"Myra has very strange tastes," Edna said, and glanced around Cameron's foyer. "I thought you were going to contact Peterson. He did wonders with our condo when we lived up here."

"Peterson didn't have time," Cameron answered, coming back from hanging up her coat and George's hat. "Peggi comes highly recommended."

Edna looked at her again. Her smile was thin. "I'm sure."

Peggi knew Edna Miller thought more was going on between Cameron and her than interior designing. She also knew it wouldn't help to deny the idea. Denials would only add more suspicions.

"Been a little nervous about the market today?" Cameron asked George.

"A little?" George led the way into Cameron's living room, leaning on his cane as he walked. "Did you see where it closed?"

"And it will be back up on Monday. You know this happens."

George settled himself in one of the wagon-wheel chairs, and Edna brushed her palm over one of the cushions of the salmon-and-turquoise-striped sofa before sitting primly on the edge. Peggi was glad for an excuse to escape. "I'll get the hors d'oeuvres."

Cameron joined her in the kitchen a moment later. "They want mineral water. Edna has always asked for a vodka martini, and I know George loves Scotch on the rocks, but tonight they want mineral water. I'm not even sure I have mineral water."

"I saw a bottle in one of these cupboards," Peggi

said, and began opening doors. She found it on the third try and handed it to him.

"Thanks." He paused, looking at her in a way that made her very uneasy. "You'll have to excuse Edna and George. Sometimes . . ." He shrugged and turned to the refrigerator.

He filled glasses with ice and poured the mineral water while Peggi heated the stuffed mushrooms under the broiler. Together they returned to the living room, each carrying a tray.

"To a rising economy." George saluted, raising his glass. Then he looked at the tray of stuffed mushrooms and the vegetables arranged around the bowl of dip. "These look good. I hope you don't mind the change in menu. My doctor says if I stay on this diet, I'll live to be a hundred."

He took one of the mushrooms, and Peggi held her breath, waiting for his reaction. She didn't notice Edna, not until the woman grabbed a napkin and spat a mouthful of carrot and dip into it.

FIVE

"Too much salt," Edna gasped.

"Too much?" Peggi took a taste and couldn't argue. The vegetable dip was too salty, and she knew why. She'd been shaken after Cameron had tasted it, too shaken to think straight. How many times had she added salt? Once? Twice? Her mind hadn't been on dip, but on Cameron and reasons why she didn't want to be interested in him. "I'll see if I can fix something else."

She left the three of them in the living room and returned to the kitchen. Nothing else in Cameron's refrigerator met the requirements of George's diet. She decided to forget the dip and began the final preparations for the meal.

As she carried the salads to the table she could hear the conversation in the living room. Cameron spoke with authority, yet his advice was carefully worded, his manner polite. She told herself it was good that she'd stayed, that she would be able to see how he functioned when he entertained clients, and that would help her

with her designs for his condominium. She tried not to
think of how she'd felt when he'd taken her scarf from
her hair or how being around him had her on edge. *I'm
not interested*, she kept telling herself. *He's just a client.*

The concept was good; it was the man who inter-
fered with the idea.

She returned to the kitchen to check on the fish,
which was cooking nicely. She was running through
her mind the few things that still needed to be done,
when she felt a presence at her back.

"Ready?" Cameron asked, close to her ear.

She stifled her gasp of surprise and glanced over her
shoulder at him. "I didn't hear you," she said, feeling a
flush of heat rise to her cheeks.

"I told them to come sit down."

She checked the sauce on the stove, turning the
heat low. "Then I guess it's time to get the show on the
road."

They filled the serving dishes with food, then Peggi
slipped off her apron and preceded him into the dining
room.

"You're joining us, how nice," Edna said. That was
the only thing she said.

George continued with his conversation, and Peggi
listened. Stocks and bonds were something she wanted
to learn more about. Maybe she didn't have the money
to invest now, but one day she hoped to be in that
position, and a nationwide economic expansion
sounded good to her. When people had money, they
thought of things like refurbishing a room or an entire
house.

"One company I think you should consider is
Wharton Ventures," Cameron suggested to George
soon after Peggi served the main course. "It's growing.

It's PE ratio is good, and *Value Line* rates it as timely and relatively low risk."

George frowned. "Didn't I read that it has a female CEO?"

"Jane Blackburn. She had a good track record with Delpart before she moved over to Wharton, and she believes in the team approach. She's as innovative as they come."

Peggi watched George shake his head; nevertheless, she wasn't prepared for his response. "She's a woman."

"So?" Peggi asked. She couldn't see what difference that made.

Both George and Cameron looked at her, and she sat a little straighter to complete her question. "So what's the problem with her being a woman?"

George answered. "It's a management problem. Sure, if she's got good men under her, she may be able to keep the company growing, but if the economy takes a turn for the worse or they run into problems . . ."

"Good men under her?" Peggi repeated, not liking the way he'd used the phrase. "And what if she has *good women* under her?"

"All the more reason not to invest in that company," George said firmly.

"Because women can't run companies?" The idea seemed too old-fashioned even to consider.

"Not major companies," George said, and glanced at his wife, smiling. "You should know as well as I do that women have trouble making decisions. While they're looking at all sides of the issue, a company can go under."

"And not looking at all sides can put a company under too."

"True, but—" George shifted his weight in his

chair, and his tone turned confiding. "Women have problems."

"Problems?"

"You know," George said, and again glanced at his wife.

Peggi sat back in her chair. "No, I don't know." She looked at Cameron. "Do you know?"

She thought she'd caught him smiling, but it vanished so quickly, she wasn't sure. His expression was serious when he said, "I think I understand what George is getting at."

"Good. Will one of you explain it to me?"

Cameron looked at George, then back at her. "I think he's referring to your mood swings."

"Ah." She did understand. "Mood swings. PMS. Those infections we get each month that Newt Gingrich feels should keep us out of the trenches. Of course, the fact that you men are often ruled by testosterone should have no bearing in this discussion."

"It's an entirely different matter," George stated.

"No, it's not." She leaned toward George. "You're saying we can't make sound judgments, can't run a company because of our hormones. I'm saying you men make just as many stupid judgments because you think with your—"

"Peggi," Cameron said firmly, interrupting her. He looked at Edna, and Peggi followed his gaze.

The older woman was picking at her fish. She smiled at Peggi. "This trout is delicious, my dear. You must give me the recipe."

"Of course," Peggi said, realizing that like it or not, the subject had been changed. "I'll be glad to."

"Your housekeeper quit?" George asked Cameron.

"She called in sick this morning. Peggi offered to help me out tonight."

George nodded, giving her no more than a glance. "I keep telling you, you need to get married."

"I'm supposed to marry Peggi."

She looked at him, startled to hear him make that statement. He smiled at her. "It was predicted, after all."

"I thought you didn't believe that psychic," she said.

"I don't. I'm just stating the facts."

"Psychic?" both George and Edna asked.

"She was on a radio talk show," Cameron explained. "I turned it on one evening by accident. Well, not really by accident. Up until that night, there was a stock report on that station."

"And," Peggi added, "Cameron felt it his obligation to call in and give his opinion on love and marriage."

He shrugged. "The woman, this psychic, said she could predict who a man would marry. I just felt someone should let her know not all men wanted to get married."

"And *she's* the woman you're supposed to marry?" George asked, pointing at Peggi.

Peggi didn't like the way he said "she" or his condescending expression. She also knew it was silly to goad the man, but she couldn't seem to help herself. "Just think, I'll be the little woman behind Cameron's success." She grinned. "Or will he be the little man behind my success?"

"You can't be serious," George said, turning back to Cameron.

"I'm not," Cameron assured him, looking very

smug about the whole thing. "It was all a farce. You tell me how some woman clear over on the East Coast can predict who I'm going to marry. If I *were* to get married. Which I'm not."

Peggi smiled and rose from her chair to begin clearing the table. "Still, the psychic said the woman he would marry would be waiting for him when he got home, and there I was, waiting for him. Wasn't I?" She ran a fingertip over the shoulder of his jacket, down his sleeve, and across the back of his hand to his plate.

"Coincidence," Cameron said, watching her take his plate. "That's all."

She kept smiling and headed for the kitchen. "If you say so."

The topic of conversation had shifted to the Millers' son by the time Peggi returned to the table. The subject of marriage was avoided, along with debates about women executives versus male. She'd figured coffee would also be off George's diet and offered a variety of herbal teas. George asked for coffee, so she made a pot.

Peggi was putting away the box of tea bags when Edna came into the kitchen carrying the dessert plates and forks. "The men took their coffee into the living room," she said, setting the plates on the counter. Lightly, she touched Peggi's arm. "If you want to get a man like Cameron, you have to learn how to handle men."

Peggi laughed at the idea. "You mean, I need to keep my mouth shut?"

"I mean a woman's power should be applied subtly. You must let a man think he's making the decisions, all the while getting exactly what you want. Since Adam and Eve, women have known this. It's a skill, but one you can learn."

Peggi shook her head, her hair swinging against the sides of her face. "I'm afraid it's not a skill I want to learn. I believe if you want something, you should simply go after it. I don't believe in game playing."

She noticed Cameron then. He stood at the buffet in the dining room, pouring more coffee. His gaze met hers and held for a moment, the power of it sending a tremor through her. Then he looked down at the cup in his hand and finished pouring the coffee.

Peggi walked with Cameron to the door as the Millers were preparing to leave, but after they'd exchanged the necessary formalities, she excused herself, saying she wanted to finish in the kitchen. Cameron brought George his hat and helped Edna with her coat. As soon as he saw the elevator door close behind the two, he shut the door to his apartment, shed his jacket and tie, and headed for the kitchen.

Peggi stood at the sink, wiping its stainless-steel sides dry with a dish towel. He leaned against the doorway, taking a second to enjoy the little wiggle of her behind that accompanied each swipe of the towel. Finally he spoke. "The dinner was good."

A jerk of her shoulders said she hadn't known he was there. Quickly, she faced him, pushing her hair back from her face. "Good in spite of the salty vegetable dip?"

He'd forgotten that. "I could have sworn it needed more salt when I tasted it."

But then, he hadn't been concentrating on dip at

the time. He'd been too distracted by her nearness. Too disturbed by the ideas running through his head.

He was disturbed now.

"I think I added too much salt," she said.

"Well besides that, you made quite an impression."

She laughed. "I'm sure. Did George warn you not to marry me, and Edna suggest you try another interior designer?"

She wasn't far off. "George said you had, ah—"

"What? A lot of gall? A big mouth? No business sense?"

"He was tactful."

"Which is more than you can say for me, right?" She shook her head. "Someday I'll learn to keep my big mouth shut."

Cameron glanced at her mouth. That was twice she'd called it big, but it wasn't. It was just the right size and shape . . . and delectably tempting.

He forced himself to look back at her eyes.

George hadn't liked what she'd had to say, but Cameron had enjoyed every minute of that conversation. He'd loved the sparks of fire he'd seen in Peggi's eyes, the rigid line of her spine. She was a fighter.

"I think you actually helped me," he said.

"How's that?" She cocked her head, her hair falling lazily over her shoulder.

"George and Edna have been badgering me for years to get married."

She laughed, the sound warm and bubbly. "And the idea of you marrying me shut them up?"

He grinned and walked over to the refrigerator. "Not a word after that conversation at the dinner table. I put some champagne in here earlier." He opened the door. "I hadn't thought about them not drinking alcohol. Join me in a glass?"

He pulled out the bottle and faced her. She'd leaned back against the counter and was watching him. "I really should be going. It's been a long day."

"A very long day." He struggled with the cork. It released with a pop, a hiss of vapor escaping into the room.

Smiling, he straightened and walked toward her. "Champagne glasses are in the cupboard to your right."

She got two long fluted glasses down and set them on the counter. "Is this how you get women? You just ignore what they say?"

"I didn't ignore what you said. I agreed with you." He poured champagne into each glass.

"Agreed and ignored."

He set the bottle down and handed one glass to her. She hesitated a moment, then took it. He picked up the other and lifted it high. "Here's to saying what you think."

She laughed and clinked her glass against his. "I'll drink to that."

He watched her take a sip. Her lipstick had worn off hours before, but her lips took on a glossy sheen when she ran the tip of her tongue over them, catching every droplet of the champagne. Not once did she look away from his face, her dark eyes reflecting her confusion. He knew she couldn't figure him out. How could she? He wasn't sure he understood himself what he was doing. Picking up the bottle, he started for the living room. "Come on. Let's talk."

She followed him, and he flicked lights out as he

passed through rooms, leaving only the chandelier in the foyer and the shimmering glow of the moonlight coming through the living-room windows to illuminate the room. "Harvest moon," he said, gazing at the silvery sphere and its reflection on the water.

"The time when the werewolves come out."

He glanced her way and smiled. The idea of werewolves conjured up images. Hair on his face and hands. Her at his mercy.

He did have a little stubble on his chin, and the hairs on his arms reached his wrists. Peggi Barnett, however, was not at his mercy.

Cameron set the bottle and his glass down on the stone-topped coffee table and sat on the sofa. Looking up at her, he patted the upholstered back. "Join me?"

She hesitated, then sat on the end, leaving ample space between them. Her look was wary. "What are you up to, Cameron?"

He chuckled. "You have a suspicious mind."

"It comes with the mood swings and PMS."

"And probably from fighting off men in trenches. You're a very attractive woman, you know." He drank from his glass, letting the bubbles play over his tongue before swallowing the wine. "If that psychic were right, I would have to compliment her taste."

"*If.*" Peggi leaned back against the sofa, gave him a cursory look, then shook her head.

"What?" he asked, not sure he wanted to know.

"That psychic couldn't have been more wrong."

"Why do you say that?"

"Because I would never marry someone like you."

"Is this reverse psychology? You say you don't want me, so therefore I'll want you."

She laughed. "You are so conceited. Why do you think every woman wants you?"

"Not every woman." He smiled and set his glass down. "But you do."

Her mouth opened, and he thought she was going to speak, then she shut it and set her glass down on the table. "You're crazy."

"Am I?" He reached out and touched her hand where it rested on her leg. She jerked her fingers back, leaving his hand to fall on her knee.

He watched her, daring her to pull away from that contact. She took in a breath and straightened her back. "I do not want you." She spoke as if she meant it, but there was a slight tremor in her voice.

"What about when you had me taste that dip?" He let his thumb stroke the silken texture of her stocking. "And when I removed your scarf? Both times I saw something in your eyes."

"The only 'something' you might have seen in my eyes were my contacts. Anything else had to be in your imagination."

He grinned. "I think we were both imagining things."

"Imagining things can get people into trouble."

"Agreed." He inched closer, bringing his other hand up to touch her chin. "You have very smooth skin."

"And you have a very smooth line." She pulled away, rising to her feet.

He watched her walk to the window. She stood with her back to him, staring out. "What's your favorite color, Mr. Slater?"

"Blue." He rose and walked over behind her. "Why?"

She didn't look his way. "I figured as long as I was here, we should continue what we started this morning."

He placed a hand on her shoulder. "And what did we start this morning?"

"Your initial consultation." A shrug and a shift of her body weight left his hand touching nothing.

"I thought you told Edna you believed in the straightforward approach, no games."

She faced him. "I do. And this is a game to you."

"You're going to say you feel nothing when we're together?"

"I feel—" She waved a hand in the air. "Nothing."

He shook his head, knowing she was lying. Gently he touched her cheek, watching the pupils of her eyes grow wider. "Liar," he whispered, then turned away and walked back to the sofa. Sitting, he poured himself more champagne.

"My favorite color is blue, I like jazz music, the view out that window, a feeling of openness, and . . ." He tried to think of other words that would describe his likes.

She interrupted his thoughts. "This morning I got the feeling you like contemporary furniture."

"Yes." He guessed he did. "I can picture this place decorated in contemporary furniture." Smiling, he looked at her. "With a beautiful woman with long legs and long blond hair lounging on the sofa."

"I'm not decorating your condo with women."

"I wasn't thinking in the plural."

Her gaze met his, and he knew she understood what he meant. Satisfied, he went on with his list. "I also like a sense of elegance, a feeling of money."

"We could always give you gold fixtures . . . paper the walls with dollar bills."

"No." He chuckled at the idea, and the Millers came to mind. "I'm also not into fur coats in September or gold-handled canes."

Her laugh was spontaneous. "Considering the temperature's not supposed to get below sixty tonight, that coat was a bit much."

Peggi came back to the sofa and sat on the end again. He leaned forward and poured her more champagne. "I want you to know, I don't agree with all George said at the dinner table."

"However, you weren't about to disagree because he's the one with the money. A lesson I need to learn, it seems."

"At least you're honest."

"I like to think I might have changed his thinking some."

Cameron shook his head. "George isn't going to change his mind because of anything you or I might say. His opinions were set decades ago—about women, politics, a number of things." Cameron leaned back against the sofa. "He thinks just like my father did."

"That a woman's place is in the kitchen?"

"That he's in control."

"But George isn't?"

"What do you think?"

Peggi thought that Edna was the one who made the final decisions in the Miller household, and that Cameron looked too damn sexy leaning back against the sofa as he was, that the hour was getting late, and she shouldn't have drunk any champagne. Her head was getting fuzzy. "I think," she said, "I should be going."

"Consultation over?"

"We seem to keep getting off the subject."

"What else do you want to know?"

"Lots of things. What you want changed. What you don't want changed."

"So ask."

If he was serious, it wouldn't hurt to get some information. Time was precious. "Do you have a pencil and paper so I can take notes?"

"In my office." He stood with the fluid motion of a man in prime physical condition. "I'll get them."

She took a deep breath the moment he left, clearing her head, and got up to snap on a light. Business, she told herself. She had to keep her mind on business, had to counter this seductive atmosphere, and had to ignore the giddy feeling that invaded her mind and body whenever he looked her way.

"Will this do?" he asked, setting a notebook and two pencils on the table.

She sat down again and flipped open the notebook. "Perfect." Picking up one of the pencils, she began her standard list of questions.

He answered each.

The carpeting, he said, had come with the condo. Hal hadn't changed it, and no, he didn't care if he had carpeting or wood floors. He also said that as far as he knew, he had no allergies to fabrics or materials, and besides blue, he liked neutral colors, especially tan and beige. "And blond," he added, looking at her hair. "Is it natural?"

"That's for me to know and you to guess."

"I'll find out," he said, his grin promising he would.

"In your dreams."

"Maybe. What else do you need to know?"

She could ask why he got her so rattled she couldn't think straight, but something less personal seemed preferable. "Do you like vertical lines or horizontal?"

"Vertical."

That didn't surprise her. Vertical lines were energetic and there was an energy around him. It kept her on edge.

She also wasn't surprised when he said he wanted as little as possible obstructing his view from the windows. In her opinion, his views of the lake and the city should be the focal points of the condo. She would plan her designs around them.

"Last question," she said, not sure if it was pure curiosity or practicality that prompted her to ask it. "Is there a woman, anyone in your life, who might have a say in how this place is to be decorated? I don't want to get started, then find out everything has to be changed because we didn't consult her . . . or him."

"No him, that's for certain," he said firmly. "And at the moment the only woman with any say in my life is you."

She noted he'd prefaced his answer with "at the moment." Tomorrow might be another matter. "If I remember correctly, that newspaper reporter wrote that your list of influential clients is equaled by your list of beautiful dates."

"As I said before, always give the impression that you're the best."

His grin was seductive, and she knew if he kept looking at her that way, she was done for. Putting down the notebook, she rose to her feet. "I hope my designs give the impression that I'm the best. I'll work on this over the weekend and give you a call sometime early next week."

"Sounds good to me." He patted the sofa again. "Don't feel you need to run off."

"If I don't go soon, I'll change back into a pumpkin. I'll just get my shoes and purse."

Peggi knew she was running from Cameron like a scared virgin, and that a man's eyes didn't hold any power, couldn't mesmerize or hypnotize. Still, she found it difficult to explain how one silly smile and a look from him could have her so flustered, or why her thoughts kept slipping from the designs of a condo to the designs of a man.

He was at his front door, waiting for her, when she returned, shoes on her feet and purse strap over her shoulder.

"Here's your change from the grocery money," she said, handing him a wad of bills and a fistful of coins.

He took the money and stuffed it into his pants pocket, then stopped her escape by blocking the door. "Aren't you curious?"

"Curious about what?"

"What a kiss would be like."

She looked up into those wicked green eyes and knew curiosity spelled danger. "Why would I be curious?" she asked, wishing her voice didn't sound so shaky.

"Because you're a woman, and women are curious." He hooked a finger under her chin. "Just as I'm a curious male."

"Cameron—" His name came out a rasp, the sound barely audible over the thudding of her heart. "We shouldn't. You said it yourself. Things could get complicated."

"No, this is to keep things from getting complicated. This is a way of defusing the pressure."

She wasn't sure she agreed with him, but she didn't move. Her legs were too heavy, her mind too frozen. With the slightest of pressure, he drew her to him, and she submitted willingly, the curiosity she'd denied all too tempting.

His eyes, she noticed, had crinkly lines at the corners. His lips were firm and slightly parted. Up close, his features blurred, just as her thoughts blurred.

Solid was her first impression. The solid feel of his chest where she pressed her hands against it, and the unyielding pressure of his mouth on hers, taking what she'd sworn she would not give yet had yearned to know.

Warmth was the next sensation.

The warmth spreading through her melted her into his arms. She was playing with fire, dancing close to the edge. She knew it, yet she flirted with the danger, giving as she received, each teasing kiss igniting a need for more.

"So tempting," he said, barely allowing her a second to catch her breath.

"So stupid."

So right.

She was drunk with the pleasure of him, her hands exploring the sheer muscular power of his arms and shoulders. A shiver of excitement shot through her as he pulled her closer, his body relaying his own reactions. She knew they had gone beyond curiosity.

Exploration blended with lust as one of his hands slid up under her jacket, finding the soft curve of a breast. His kisses became more penetrating, more demanding, until the thrust of his tongue proclaimed a stronger desire.

The need ricocheting through her was too frightening to consider. Stunned, she drew back, her breathing shallow and ragged, her thoughts in a jumble.

"Stay," he said softly. "Spend the night with me."

"No. I can't—we shouldn't." She wanted to run before she changed her mind, to flee the temptation.

"Let's get this behind us."

"No," she repeated, her body shaking.

"It's going to tear at us every time we're together."

"We can control it," she insisted. "I can control it." She had to.

Cameron wasn't sure he could. The need within him was stronger than he'd ever known. Too strong. He drew in a deep breath, watching her. The emotions he'd experienced were unnerving. Kisses shouldn't be so explosive, shouldn't leave him weak and confused.

It wasn't going to work, he realized. He couldn't keep her on as his interior designer. He'd been right when he'd told her things got complicated when you got involved with someone you worked with. Curiosity had banished his good business sense. "I really should be going," she said, not moving.

"I'll walk you to your car." And out of his life.

"No." She shook her head. "I'll be fine. I'm just down the street. Your doorman can keep an eye on me."

"I insist." He was determined to be the gentleman to the end, though he knew in the end she would hate him.

"No," she repeated firmly, raising her chin and staring him in the eyes. "Let's leave it at this."

He knew then that she knew. His call to her shop in

the morning would merely be a formality. He would give his excuses, she would politely accept them, and they would go their separate ways.

She smiled tentatively and held out her hand. "It's been an interesting day. . . . An interesting week."

SIX

The thumping noise penetrated her dream until Peggi realized it was a reality. Cracking open her eyes and lifting her head from the pillow, she gazed at the clock by her bed. The oversized numbers read "7:10." Too darned early to be waking up on a Saturday morning.

"Go away!" she yelled, and let her head fall back on the pillow, her eyes once again closing.

"Peggi!" The gravelly male voice came from the opposite side of the door. "I need to see you."

Her eyes snapped open, the room around her coming into hazy nearsighted focus. Light was filtering through the blinds on her windows, catching the bright splashes of orange and yellow that accented her studio apartment. Pushing back the blankets, she sat on the edge of the bed and combed her fingers through her hair.

She remembered bits and pieces from the night before: her argument with George Miller, Edna Miller's advice about manipulating men, Cameron opening a bottle of champagne. He'd offered her a drink, and she'd taken it. That had been her big mistake. From that point on, things got confused in her memory. The questions she'd asked him blended with the looks he'd given her, looks and smiles that had slowly seduced her, until finally she'd succumbed to his kisses.

Oh, what kisses.

She ran her tongue over her lips, the taste of him lingering.

"Peggi?" The thumping started again.

"Coming," she yelled back. "Give me a minute."

She didn't have a robe. Her old favorite had turned into shreds, and she hadn't replaced it yet. She did have an afghan draped over the back of her cream-colored sofa. Wrapping it around her so it covered her shorty nightgown, she grabbed her glasses from the table and, barefoot, headed for the door.

"Who is it?" she asked, though she knew perfectly well who was on the other side. Never would she forget his voice, the persuasion of his lips, the hardness of his body. Never would she forget the temptation . . . or the frustration.

"Cameron," he answered. "I need to talk to you."

"It's seven o'clock in the morning."

"I know. I'm sorry to wake you, but I have an eight o'clock tee time. I'll only take a minute."

He didn't sound sorry. He sounded decisive and commanding and fully awake. She struggled to reach that state.

The chain and dead bolt released, she opened the door and stepped back. He stood in the hallway, dominating the space, his hair slightly tousled, a pale blue sweater covering a white polo shirt, his trousers casual and sneakers on his feet. He could have stepped from the pages of a men's sport ad. She felt like a street urchin.

Again, she ran her fingers through her hair, pushing it back from her face and trying to release the tangles of sleep. The afghan slipped, baring the lacy pink cotton that covered her shoulder. His gaze dropped to that point, then lower. With a sweep of those green eyes, he took her in, and she felt the chill of the morning give way to a deep arousing heat.

"May I come in?" he asked, stepping forward.

He walked past her and into her apartment as though he owned the place. She'd thought she wouldn't see him again, yet here he was. Slowly, she closed her door.

Cameron took a moment to glance around her apartment. He hadn't expected a studio. A small sofa and easy chair occupied one corner, a circular table and four kitchen chairs another. The kitchenette was compact—a breakfast counter projecting into the room— while a raised platform separated her sleeping area. Everything was color and light, creams and ivory accented by touches of green, yellow, and orange. Even the sheets covering her double bed repeated the color scheme.

"I like," he said, amazed by how she'd combined color and space to create a sense of energy and openness. What could have been a drab, cramped room in a low-cost apartment building was a showcase of simple good taste.

"I call it home," she said, also glancing around.

Her glasses were slightly askew, her hair mussed, and her makeup nonexistent. She looked like a woman who'd just gotten out of bed, and from the looks of her bed and what she'd said, he should feel guilty for waking her.

He didn't.

Sleep wasn't something he'd gotten a lot of the night before. Physically and mentally frustrated, he'd tossed and turned in bed, his thoughts replaying all that had happened in the hours before . . . in the days before. He didn't believe in psychic predictions, but he had wanted Peggi, and that desire—that actual need—had disturbed him. Before she'd left, he'd decided it wouldn't work.

Around five A.M., though, he'd considered the legal ramifications of firing her. That was when he'd changed his mind.

He knew enough about the law to realize he'd be treading dangerous ground if he let her go after having propositioned her and being turned down. He didn't need a sexual-harassment suit. What he needed was to talk to her.

"You left these," he said, holding three cookbooks toward her.

"Oh—I forgot all about them." She reached for the books and the afghan slipped lower, giving him an ever-more-enticing view of her shoulder and the hint of one breast. She caught him staring, her gaze meeting his for the briefest of moments before she looked away. An adjustment, and she had the afghan back in place and the books under her arm.

"Thank you." She carried them to the table. "I seem to be making a habit of leaving things at your place."

"It's one way to make sure you see me again."

Her eyebrows arched, creating golden accents behind her glasses. "Is that what you think?"

"It's been done before."

"You forget, I don't play games."

"All women play games."

She cocked her head. "Why are you here, Cameron?" Her glance went back to the books. "Certainly not to return those. Not at this hour in the morning."

"I wanted to talk to you." An hour ago it had seemed paramount that he see her right away. Now that he was here, he wondered at the wisdom of his actions. "About last night—"

He stopped, not quite sure how to go on. Being in the same room as her bed, knowing she had little on under the afghan, his thoughts were more jumbled than before. Had he woken up with her by his side that morning, things would have been different.

Then, again, maybe not.

"I was out of line last night," he went on. "I shouldn't have—"

When he stopped this time, Peggi grinned. As improbable as it seemed, Chicago's man-about-town was groping for words. She finished for him. "You shouldn't have been so curious?"

She caught his quick glance at her mouth. "I don't want you feeling there's any pressure on you, one way or the other. For me to have taken our relationship beyond business was foolish."

Foolish but exciting. "I understand . . . and agree."

"Whether I go with your designs, or decide not to hire you, should be a decision unclouded by other factors."

She nodded, beginning to understand. "Afraid I might slap a sexual-harassment suit on you if you turn me down?"

The slight lift of his eyebrows told her that was exactly what he feared. He'd certainly scurried over here early enough. His position was untenable, and he knew it.

"Let's see," she said. "You ask me to sleep with you, I refuse, and you turn down my designs." She nodded again as though seriously considering the idea. "Yes, I think I would have a case."

"I wouldn't turn down your designs for that reason," he said gruffly. "What happened last night was between you and me."

"And whose condo are we talking about my redecorating?"

"Mine." He let out a frustrated sigh.

"Has you worried, doesn't it?" She turned away from him and started for her kitchen area. "Would you like some coffee?"

"I don't have time." He stayed where he was. "I won't accept something I don't like just to keep you out of court."

"I wouldn't expect you to." She turned on the tap and grabbed her coffee carafe. Keeping the afghan in place became an impossibility, and it slipped once more as she filled the coffee carafe with water. Her back to Cameron, Peggi hoped he couldn't see much from where he stood.

What Cameron could see enticed him. He wasn't sure if she was teasing him with her body or trying to be modest, but her efforts to cover herself were failing. Her pale pink cotton nightgown did little to hide the silhouette of her body. Starting below the point where her hair waved over her shoulder blades, he saw the distinct outline of her torso.

He knew from holding her last night that she didn't

have a weight problem. Her body had been firm against his, yet womanly soft. He also knew if she turned to pour that water into the coffeemaker, he was going to see more than he probably should under the circumstances. "Why don't you let me help," he said, coming up behind her.

He heard her quick intake of breath and knew his nearness had surprised her. She released the carafe to him and grabbed the afghan, gathering it under her armpits. Only then did she face him.

His downward glance brought the discovery that her efforts to cover herself had revealed more than before. The creamy thigh now exposed to his view looked velvety soft, the small butterfly tattoo on her hip tempting.

He grinned, and she noticed the direction of his gaze. Quickly, she adjusted the afghan, once again concealing the butterfly and her body from his view. Shaking her hair back from her face, she looked at him as if daring a comment. Only the rosy pink of her cheeks revealed her embarrassment.

He kept the smile, but made no comment about the butterfly. He'd seen more than he should have, and was having problems of his own. Physical problems. He needed to get his mind on other matters. "Where do you keep the coffee?"

"In there." She pointed at a cupboard. "But I can—"

He opened the cupboard and took down the canister and a filter. "How much do you usually use?"

She gave in, stepping back. "There's a scoop inside. One per cup. How did you know where I lived?"

"I called your shop this morning. I thought you lived there. I got your answering machine, then in the middle of my message, your partner picked up the phone."

"Darlene was up?"

"Up and very talkative. She said she was going to an auction this morning. Somewhere near Oak Park. She also explained that you didn't live there, only she did, and if I wanted to see you, I should just stop by here. Since your place wasn't far off my route to the club, that's what I decided to do."

"At seven in the morning."

"Obviously you're not as early a riser as your partner."

"Not on Saturdays." Especially not on this Saturday. Peggi doubted she'd gotten a total of three hours sleep the night before. She had spent the time tossing and turning . . . and remembering the kisses they'd shared.

The coffee began to brew, and he moved away. "You do understand my concern about last night, don't you?"

"I understand." She leaned back against the counter, keeping the afghan secure. "You know, it's funny, but last night I did think you would back out."

"Did you." He walked out of the kitchen area, wandering into the section she considered her living room. "You don't have much room to move around here, do you?"

"I can't say my place is as spacious as yours." She watched him walk over to the two photographs she had hanging on her wall.

"Your family?" he asked, pointing to one of the pictures.

"That's my sister, Dana, her husband, Ted, and my nephew, Joel, when he was four."

"The nephew with the tonsils?"

She nodded. "Missing tonsils now."

"He's doing all right?"

"Fine. Eating tons of ice cream, according to Dana."

Cameron smiled. "I remember when I had mine out. My mother promised ice cream." And he'd never gotten it.

His gaze switched to the next picture. A middle-aged couple stood on a beach, a sea of clear blue water behind them. The woman looked like Peggi, tall, willowy, and blond. On the other hand, Peggi didn't look a bit like the short, dark-haired man. "Your parents?"

"My mother. Kevin is my stepfather. My father died when I was two." Peggi walked over to where Cameron stood. "I don't remember my real father, and Mom married Kevin when I was eight, so he's almost like a father. They live up in Wisconsin now." She grinned. "And are very happy. Both my mother and my sister have good marriages."

She'd stressed the words "very happy," and he got her point. "As far as you know, they have good marriages," he argued. "But what's on the surface isn't always reality."

"Such bitterness." She clucked her tongue, scolding his cynicism. "Let me guess. Your parents got divorced."

He shook his head.

"Constantly fought?"

Again he shook his head. She was like most women, wanting an answer for why he was against marriage. He wasn't about to explain, at least no more than he'd told that psychic. The reason was too complex—and too simple.

"My parents got along fine," he said. "In fact, my father doted on my mother. As far as he was concerned, the sun rose and set in her. And she worried about him all the time. She was devastated when he died."

"Your father died?"

"Oh yeah." It still infuriated him. "Cancer."

"I'm sorry. Recently?"

"No, when I was sixteen."

Peggi wanted to reach out and touch him, let him know she understood his loss, but she held back. Touching seemed too intimate, too dangerous. She kept her reaction bland. "Cancer is so terrible."

"Especially when it doesn't have to be."

There was an anger to his words that she didn't understand. Unspoken accusations. "Meaning?"

"Meaning if he'd gotten out of the factory where he worked when he had the chance, he would probably be alive today. The company may say the chemicals my father handled had nothing to do with his death, but I'll never be convinced."

His brief flash of emotion disappeared, and Cameron's expression again turned guarded. "So we both have fathers who died, and mothers who remarried." The snort he gave was cynical. "Marriage seems to be a favorite pastime of your sex."

"The species is supposed to propagate and multiply," she said. "Not live a solitary life."

"One doesn't need to get married to propagate." He glanced toward her bed.

She noticed. "For me, sex without commitment is—well, just sex."

"Ah yes, but I have a feeling it would be damned good sex." He smiled suggestively. "Anytime you change your mind, let me know."

"Don't hold your breath."

"Oh, I won't." He glanced at his watch, then stepped back, toward her door. "I've got to go. You'll call me when those designs are ready?"

She nodded. "Should be sometime next week."

Cameron felt guilty when he left Peggi's apartment. He'd told her it didn't matter if she slept with him or not. What he hadn't told her—couldn't tell her—was that seeing her again had only reinforced his decision to say no to her designs.

How could he work with her? She kept him in a constant state of confusion; she got him telling her more about himself than he ever told others. He hadn't meant to say anything about his father. There was no need.

Once at the country club, he tried to block her from his thoughts. The effort was futile. One minute he would remember the kiss they'd shared the night before, how she'd tasted and how she'd felt. The next he was mentally rehashing their arguments. He couldn't keep his mind on the running conversation his three golfing buddies were holding, not until Mitch brought up Peggi's name. Then Cameron listened.

"You ought to see the lovely our Don Juan here has hired to redecorate his condo," Mitch said to Charlie McMillan and Leo Steinfeld.

Cameron corrected Mitch. "I haven't officially hired her."

"Good-looker, though?" Charlie asked, giving Cameron a knowing grin.

"Legs up to here," Mitch answered, holding a hand up to his chin. "Long blond hair." He paused and looked at Cameron. "Though that may not be natural."

Cameron remembered his glimpse of hip and thigh when Peggi had pulled the afghan up to her chin. He'd seen the butterfly tattoo, and a little more. Smiling, he looked at Mitch. "It's natural."

"Aha! Our man scores again." Mitch shook his head. "I don't know how you do it. Here I am, healthy, not too bad looking, and I have a growing law practice. I'm finally, once again, in good financial straits, and I'm perfectly willing to get married. But do I have women throwing themselves at me? Do I find an interior decorator who looks like a *Sports Illustrated* swimsuit model?"

Cameron chuckled at his friend's supposed dilemma. "I didn't know you were looking for an interior decorator who looked like a *Sports Illustrated* swimsuit model. That bank manager you were with last week wasn't bad."

"Not bad? You want to talk about boring?" Mitch stretched out the word. "I took her to the comedy club last night, and she barely cracked a smile."

"Now, that is bad," Leo said.

"My wife always catches on to the jokes an hour later," Charlie said, grumbling. "If she catches on at all. The longer we're married, the less of a sense of humor she has. You're the smart one, Cam. Enjoy them for a while, then move on."

"Just like your uncle, right?" Mitch said. His uncle had played golf with all three of them on different occasions. "It's the thrill of the chase for you guys."

"I don't know about 'thrill,'" Cameron said.

Leo chuckled. "To hear John talk, it's a thrill. How's he doing, anyway? Still raking in the millions?"

"Doing well. His company's still ranked by *Value Line* as one of the best buys."

"Have you talked to him since that talk show?" Mitch asked. "Checked to see if he's been contacted by his soul mate?"

"Soul mate?" Charlie and Leo repeated.

Mitch related the story, beginning with the market report being replaced by a talk show. He managed to drag the story out to the fourteenth hole, embellishing on it here and there. Finally, he ended with Peggi being in Cameron's condo, waiting for him, just as the psychic had predicted.

"So you've met your soul mate," Leo said, grinning.

"I hope not." Cameron laughed at the idea. "She could ruin my career. She had dinner at my place last night with George and Edna Miller, and I thought she was going to declare war on old George when he stated that women weren't as competent as men."

"*The* George Miller of Mill-Tech Corporation?" Charlie asked.

"The one and only."

Mitch laughed. "Considering how she laid into you the other day, I'm sure she had your old boy on the defensive."

"George told me I needed my head examined if I got involved with her."

"Yep." Mitch nodded smugly. "You two are a perfect match."

"No way."

"She'd keep your life interesting."

"I can find other ways to keep my life interesting."

The three of them looked at Cameron, grinning, and he shook his head. "Forget it. I am *not* getting married, and that's that." He zeroed in on Mitch. "I don't see why you're so keen on jumping back into that state anyway. You've been run through the wringer once. Why repeat the situation?"

Mitch kept grinning and walked up to the tee. " 'Cause when it was good, it was very good."

Peggi finished her third cup of coffee and closed the most recent issue of *Architectural Digest*. One thing about getting up early, she'd accomplished a lot that morning. Her weekly vacuuming and dusting were behind her, the bills were paid, and she'd caught up on her reading. Her head was brimming with fresh ideas, and she was ready to head to the shop and start work on the designs for Cameron's condo.

Darlene had said she didn't expect to be back from that auction until late in the afternoon, but Wednesday they'd hired a woman to work Saturdays, and since she hadn't called, Peggi assumed everything was going well at the shop.

She'd no sooner thought that than the telephone rang.

She picked up the receiver, ready to answer a simple question. What she heard was a panicky, "Peg?"

She immediately recognized Darlene's voice. "What's the matter? Where are you?"

"At the shop. My car wouldn't start, so I didn't go to the auction. Peg, I got a call this morning."

Sighing, Peggi relaxed. Darlene was being her usual dramatic self. She should have been an actress. "From Cameron, right? I know. He stopped by."

"Not Cameron." Darlene paused, and Peggi heard her suck in a breath. "He's back."

"He?" Darlene's brevity said volumes, and Peggi didn't think she was acting. "You mean . . . ?"

"Jim."

Peggi could understand Darlene's agitation. Jim Lawrence had left her more than three years ago. One month after the death of their baby, he'd taken off. He'd needed to "find" himself. Or so he'd said, when he finally made contact. Since then, Jim had called occasionally, each time upsetting Darlene, but he'd never come back to Chicago as far as Peggi knew.

"He's at his parents' house," Darlene said. "He wants to see me. Peg, what am I going to do?"

"What do you want to do?" Peggi knew exactly what she would like to do to Jim Lawrence. In her opinion, any man who left is wife when she was still dealing with the loss of a baby—any man so wrapped up in himself that he couldn't see how he was ruining someone else's life—should be tarred and feathered and hung by his toes.

"I don't know," Darlene admitted. "I want to see him. We need to get things settled. But—"

"But what?"

"I'm afraid . . . afraid of how I'll feel if I do see him. Oh, Peggi, am I crazy?"

"Probably," Peggi said. "Men make us that way."

"Well, one thing for sure," Darlene said with a sigh. "No more waiting. He's here."

SEVEN

Monday, Cameron stood on the sidewalk outside of a two-story brownstone. The words PDQ INTERIORS were painted on the window. Hanging below was a small sign that said OPEN.

Of course the place was open, he told himself. Why wouldn't it be open? It was two o'clock in the afternoon. Most businesses were open; most people were working. He should be at his own office making calls and catching up on paperwork, not halfway across town staring at an interior designer's window.

With a shake of his head, he forced his gaze away. Two middle-aged women walked past and smiled. He knew he looked out of place. PDQ Interiors was flanked by dress boutiques and novelty shops. Down the street a tour bus was parked.

The area was a woman's shopping paradise. There was absolutely no reason for him to be there. Peggi hadn't called and asked him to stop by. Driving over after lunch had been a spur-of-the-moment decision.

All morning, she'd been haunting his thoughts. Every time he'd started to read a report, he'd remembered something about her. Her cooking dinner in his kitchen. Her argument with George Miller. Her standing by her coffeemaker, afghan wrapped around her nightgown and that creamy-white thigh with the butterfly exposed to his view, taunting him.

He wanted to sever all ties with her, and he wanted to see her again. To put it succinctly, he wasn't sure what he wanted. He wasn't sure what he knew, either, other than that he'd remembered during lunch that he hadn't paid her for the consultation or for all she'd done Friday. He could have put a check in the mail, but if he delivered it . . .

Straightening his tie, he walked away from his Lexus and up the steps. The bell above the door rang at his entry, and he paused. The painting hanging behind a statue caught his attention. There was energy in the spattering of colors. A boldness.

He liked it.

In the room to his left, a woman in her early thirties was thumbing through a sample book, while in the rooms to his right several women milled about, looking at the merchandise on display. Chatter permeated the shop, along with the sounds coming from a television set that was showing various room arrangements.

What Cameron didn't see was Peggi.

Then he heard her voice amid the others. More vigorous. More lilting. And more concerned.

"No, of course not," she said.

He stepped into the front room on the right, bringing her into view. A different woman from the one he'd left Saturday morning stood behind the counter, telephone in hand. The plaid jumper she wore was red-orange and black, her white long-sleeved cotton blouse surprisingly demure, and the twist she'd pulled her hair into quite sophisticated. Only one stray lock dangling recklessly by the side of her face destroyed the chic image. With each shake of her head, it slapped against her cheek.

"I can't believe it," she said into the phone. "No, that would ruin the look. I'll be over just as soon as I can."

A crash at the back of the shop jerked her gaze in that direction. She looked right past him, but gave no indication that she'd seen him.

"It just slipped out of my hand," an older woman said, looking down at a shattered vase.

"Are you going to help me?" a woman standing in front of Peggi asked sharply. "Or just ignore me?"

As Peggi's gaze switched back to that customer Cameron heard the woman from the first room call out, "Can someone help me in here?"

The place was a madhouse. Peggi wasn't going to have time to see him, wouldn't be pleased if he bothered her to deliver a check he could have easily mailed. The smart move would be to get out of there and back to his office.

It took Peggi another minute to get Velma Gose off the phone. Upset hardly described the woman, and Peggi could understand why. She needed to get over to the Gose house, and quickly. But how to leave with Darlene gone and a shop full of customers?

What a day for Darlene to disappear.

"Can you help me now?" the woman standing directly in front of her asked, slapping an embroidered towel down on the counter.

"I'm sorry." Peggi smiled politely and glanced around the shop. She'd seen Cameron earlier, all fancily dressed in a tailored gray suit, blue shirt, and red print tie and looking as sexy as ever. He'd stood out in a shop full of women.

He would stand out anywhere.

She didn't see him now, though. Not a man was in sight, and she wondered if she'd been hallucinating. She'd been having a lot of wild thoughts since meeting Cameron Slater. An hallucination would be right in line.

Picking up the towel on the counter, she checked the price tag. The day was turning absolutely insane. Where was Darlene?

They'd talked just the night before, Darlene all excited and dramatically saying that Jim was a changed man. Peggi wasn't all that convinced. Or maybe she was just getting jaded.

Darlene hadn't said anything about not being around today. There'd been no call, no note. Nothing.

Two more women made purchases and left, the shop emptying as quickly as it had filled. It was when the decorating-tips video on the television ended that Peggi heard a deep, gravelly voice coming from the parlor area. So she hadn't been hallucinating earlier. Leaving the cash register, she ventured in that direction.

Cameron stood by one of the windows, an attractive woman in her early thirties by his side. "Ah, you're free," he said, looking her way. "I was just telling Alice that you can do only one room, if that's all she wants."

"Of course," Peggi said, smiling pleasantly and walking toward them.

She didn't want to care that he was with another

woman. Why should she care? He was merely a client. That he'd kissed her passionately Friday night and had asked her to sleep with him meant nothing. He was a playboy. Playboys kissed women, collected them like trophies. Only an idiot would let herself care.

Peggi took in a bracing breath. She was an idiot.

Alice only half smiled as she neared. "Cameron said you charge fifty dollars for a consultation?"

"The fee is applied to your costs if you hire me; otherwise it covers my time and travel."

"Is that reasonable?" Alice asked him. "I'm just so naive about things like this."

"It's customary," he assured her.

"I hate being divorced . . . having to make decisions on my own." Alice sighed, then looked back up at him. She didn't bat her eyelashes, but she came close, and her voice was sugary sweet when she asked him, "Could we go somewhere and talk? Maybe over a cup of coffee? There's a place just down the block. I'd feel so much better if I had some pointers before I go ahead with this."

Peggi doubted it was pointers Alice wanted from Cameron. She was also beginning to think he hadn't brought her.

His smile was charming, but he shook his head. "Sorry. Maybe another time. As soon as I'm through here, I have to get back to my office."

"You say your office is downtown?" Alice smiled. "Maybe I'll stop by there sometime. I could use financial advice."

The woman was being so obvious, it was sickening, but Peggi said nothing, not until Alice had left the shop. Then she mimicked the woman. "You say your office is downtown? Maybe I'll stop by sometime."

He grinned, stepping toward her. "You do that."

His nearness drew her to attention, the mimicry leaving her voice. "You do attract the women."

"Jealous?"

"Me?" She forced a laugh and stepped back. "Why would I be jealous?"

His grin didn't go away. "Good question."

Disturbed by how easily he could arouse her, she turned and walked over to the front window. As she flipped the Open sign to Closed her hand shook. She hoped he didn't notice.

"Closing because of me?" he asked.

She faced him again. "Don't flatter yourself. I'm closing because I have to run to a client's and there's no one but me here to tend shop."

"So I noticed." He looked around. "Where's your partner?"

"That's another good question."

"Don't you have any backup help?"

She bristled at the suggestion that she wasn't better prepared. "Yes, we have backup help, but it just so happens we normally don't need anyone on Mondays, and our backup help is not available today."

"So you're going to close. What do you do if another tour bus stops?"

"Miss it." What else could she do? "Tour buses usually don't come on Mondays. That one was unexpected."

"All right, then." He rephrased his question. "What do you do if a customer like Alice shows up while you're closed?"

"Either she comes back when we're open or we lose her business," Peggi said, not sure PDQ Interiors would get Alice's business anyway. Cameron was more likely to score there.

"My point is—"

"Don't bother making one." She didn't need to hear what she already knew. "What else can I do? They're putting up the wrong wallpaper in Mrs. Gose's den. I've got to get over there."

She was a damsel in distress, and Cameron saw no choice but to help. "Your 'what else' is that you could hire me to watch the shop for you while you're gone."

"You?" She cocked her head, pure disbelief shadowing her eyes. "You said you had to get back to your office."

"I changed my mind. You got me out of a bind last Friday. Now it's my turn."

"You said you'd pay for my help last Friday," she reminded him. "What you quoted was a nice sum of money. All I can offer is minimum wage."

He smiled at the idea of earning minimum wage. "We'll work something out."

"Something?"

From her expression, he knew where her mind had gone. "I wasn't thinking of sex. Although . . ."

He knew what her response would be even before it reached her lips. Stepping forward, he touched a finger to her mouth and stopped her from saying anything. "Don't worry. Between us, it's business only. Right?"

"Right," she agreed, her gaze locked with his until he dropped his hand back to his side. Even then, her voice was a little shaky. "Business only."

That left him to come up with an alternative idea. "How about dinner sometime, then. You choose the restaurant. Micky D on up. Fair enough?"

"You're serious?" Her surprise was evident.

"I'm serious. But you'd better show me how to work your cash register before you leave."

"I may be gone for a couple of hours."

Two hours that he should be spending at his office. He had to be insane. "No problem," he said, smiling.

"On Mondays, it's usually really quiet. What you walked into a bit ago was unusual. You'll probably get bored."

"If so, I've got a *Barron's* out in my car that I can read."

"And we have the videos that you can watch, or you can look through the furniture catalogs and fabric sample books here in the library." She pointed toward the back of the room. Near her drafting table, rows of binders filled a bookcase. "They might give you some ideas."

She started out of the room, then stopped. "I hate to ask this, but is there any chance you could sweep up that broken vase?"

He chuckled. He was not only working for his supper, he was doing janitorial work. "Consider it done."

The decision made, she became a bundle of energy, showing him the basics of the cash register, giving him a quick rundown of their procedures and a phone number where he could reach her if necessary. Then she grabbed her coat and purse. She paused before going out the door. "Thanks, and I promise more than a hamburger at a fast-food restaurant for this."

As the door closed behind her the reality of what he'd just agreed to do hit him. Here he was, tending a shop he knew nothing about, ignoring his own work and clients, all because one leggy blonde had him panting for her body.

It was crazy.

Sweeping up the broken base took all of three minutes. After that, he wandered around the shop, familiarizing himself with the merchandise on display and studying the paintings hanging on the walls. Except for the one hanging in the entryway, all were titled and had the name of the artist and the price. And, of course, it was the one in the entryway that he liked the best.

Two women came in, browsed around, then left. He watched the video on decorating tips for a while, found it pretty basic, considered going out and getting his *Barron's*, then changed his mind. Going through furniture catalogs wasn't a bad idea. He really didn't know that much about furniture or interior decor. Growing up in a home where bargain-priced furniture, K mart prints, and cheap ceramic statues were considered fashionable, he hadn't developed sophisticated tastes. The homes of his clients were what he wanted to imitate; the homes of his uncle.

Cameron walked into the room where Peggi kept her catalogs, picked up a couple, and carried them back to the cash register.

Peggi pulled her coat closer, glad she'd brought it with her, and tried to push the strands of hair slapping across her eyes back into her twist. Though it still had been warm a few days earlier, fall was definitely in the air now, the walnut trees already losing their leaves and the gray skies above threatening rain.

At the steps to the shop, she paused. A black Lexus parked on the street caught her eye, and she knew without a doubt that it belonged to Cameron. She'd also bet the LS was the most expensive model.

Her tastes in men had certainly risen a notch. Brian had been a struggling college student, Sean had been strapped with child-support payments, and Craig had been out of work when she'd met him. Not that being attracted to a man with money was any wiser than being attracted to poor men, not when none of them was interested in marriage.

She didn't want to be attracted to Cameron. Not physically. Not mentally. Not in any way. Hadn't she vowed to stay clear of men who wanted affairs and nothing more?

But how did you stay clear of a man like Cameron?

His offer to watch the shop had taken her completely by surprise. It had been so out of character. The article she'd read about him had portrayed him as a playboy, a man-about-town, not a knight in shining armor. He was a user, a taker; his conversation with the psychic had made that clear.

Users didn't help people.

Cameron was more dangerous than she'd thought, Peggi realized. She could deal with a playboy. Sex appeal could be ignored. But how did you ignore a man who came to your rescue?

Unsure how to answer the question, she walked up the steps and entered her shop. The outside door shut hard against the pressure of the wind, the bell above ringing loudly. Cameron looked up from the catalog he had spread open on the counter, and Peggi knew that ignoring the sex appeal wasn't going to be all that easy, either.

He'd taken off his suit jacket and had loosened his tie. The result was a half-civilized look that promised excitement, whether it be in a boardroom or a bedroom. A woman would have to be dead not to think

about the possibility of making love with a man like
him.

Peggi certainly wasn't dead.

"I'm back," she said, walking toward him. "How'd
it go?"

"Fine. Quiet." He smiled and stood straighter, flexing his shoulders. "How'd it go with you?"

"Not great. They did mess up the wallpaper order.
That's going to put us back a couple of weeks."

"Does this happen often?"

"Often enough to be irritating." She dropped her
purse by the counter and unbuttoned her coat. "Did
Darlene call, by any chance?"

He shook his head and handed her three slips of
paper. "These were the only calls you received. Nothing terribly important."

She glanced over the messages, silently agreeing
with him. "You make a good secretary."

"Something I've always wanted to be." He took a
sip from a mug of coffee. "Hope you don't mind, but I
went into the kitchen and made a pot of coffee. In fact,
if you want some . . ." He glanced toward the
kitchen.

She shook her head. She was jittery enough simply
being around him. She didn't need caffeine.

"Your partner just up and left?" he asked, leaning
on the counter and cradling the mug in his hands.

"Her husband came back Saturday."

"The longtime-absent husband?"

"The one and only husband. I imagine she's with
him." Peggi just didn't know where.

"And you're not pleased?"

That was an understatement. "As far as I'm concerned, she should tell the guy to take a hike."

"I thought you were the one who believed in love and marriage."

"He deserted her for three years." She still couldn't understand that, couldn't understand Darlene taking him back. But then, there were a lot of things she didn't understand. Cameron in particular. "You probably approve. It's your game. The old 'love 'em and leave 'em' scenario."

"I don't love them and leave them."

"Don't you?"

She thought she caught a look of guilt before he glanced down at the catalog again, and she knew she'd pushed too far once more. It was time to change the subject.

"See anything you like?"

He looked back up. "As a matter of fact, yes."

He flipped back two pages and pointed at a picture of a creamy-white sofa. She smiled. His choice wasn't far from what she'd had in mind for his place. The difference was the manufacturer. "Leave it to you to pick the most expensive sofa made . . . and about the hardest to get. That's Italian leather, Cameron. Imported."

"Meaning it would take a long time to get here?"

She nodded. "Cost no problem?"

He didn't hesitate. "No problem."

"Then I'll make a few calls. Color?"

"You're the designer."

"I think the cream would be good. It would fit what I've been working on."

"How are you coming with the designs?" he asked, stepping around the counter to her side.

She'd felt more at ease with a counter between

them. Now he was too close. She edged back. "They're coming."

"How soon will I be able to see them?"

"Very soon. Two, three days."

"Good."

He touched her shoulders, and she sucked in a breath. "Wouldn't you like to take off your coat? Stay awhile?"

"Of course—sure." It was ridiculous to leave it on, as warm as it was in the shop . . . as warm as she was with him near.

He helped her, stepping behind her to draw the sleeves down her arms. She felt his breath on her hair, his fingers rubbing against the cotton of her shirt and leaving a heated trail. "I like nice things," he said.

She wasn't sure if they were still talking about furniture. "Nice things can be expensive."

"I can afford them."

Her coat was off, but he didn't move, and neither did she. "It must be nice," she said, "having lots of money."

"I haven't always had money." He chuckled, the rumble deep and oh so near. "It's amazing how much more women like you when you have money."

"Money's never mattered that much to me."

"Really?" He touched her arm, turning her toward him. Her coat went on top of the counter, freeing his hands. He stood so close, she could see the buttons of his shirt rise and fall with each breath he took. His smile was wicked. "Why do I find that hard to believe?"

"I don't know why because I mean it." She tried to keep her voice steady, but the way he was looking at her, she found it difficult. "All I want is enough money to live comfortably."

"And how comfortable are you right now?"

Not comfortable at all, she wanted to say, her legs shaking and her heart racing. She kept her answer enigmatic. "I think you know."

He studied her, his gaze intense, then he stepped back and glanced around the shop. "I'm glad I offered to help out this afternoon. It's been an interesting experience. In the last few years I've developed an idea of what I like and don't like, but—"

He looked at her. "I still remember the first time I visited my uncle after he'd gone into the computer-chip business. I was twelve. He'd just bought a house in Menlo Park, and he flew me out there for a week's visit. What an experience. I'd never been on an airplane before or in a house with that many bedrooms and bathrooms."

"Really nice?" Peggi asked, fascinated by Cameron's smile. It was softer than most of his smiles. Warmer.

She doubted he even realized he was smiling.

"That place was fantastic," he said. "At least, to me it was. Shoot, I'd grown up in an old two-story brick house in uptown Chicago. This place was a palace by comparison. It had a long, circular drive, a lawn that my uncle practiced putting on, and a swimming pool shaped like a kidney. The house itself was decorated in a western motif, but not like what I have at my place. This was classy."

He formed the okay sign with his fingers, and Peggi grinned. She had a feeling it was his memories of his uncle's house that had led him to the Southwestern motif in his condo. "You're pretty close to your uncle, aren't you?"

"Yeah." Cameron shrugged and smiled. "He's only fourteen years older than I am, and when I was little, he spent a lot of time over at our house. Sometimes my folks would get his girlfriend Clare to baby-sit, and Uncle John would come over too."

Cameron chuckled. "Not that my mother ever knew he was there. She would have had one of her spells if she'd known what Uncle John and Clare were doing."

That piqued Peggi's curiosity. "I take it Uncle John and Clare weren't just watching you."

Again, Cameron laughed. "Hardly. Of course, back then I wasn't old enough to figure out what was going on. I know I was four and that Uncle John and Clare were seniors in high school. I remember Uncle John telling me Clare had a sore back and he and she were going to go into the other room so he could massage her back . . . and not to bother them."

"A sore back, huh?"

Cameron nodded, grinning. "Chronic."

"So what happened to Clare?"

"I really don't know." He shrugged. "After he graduated from high school, my uncle took off to see the world. I remember the night of his graduation party. That's when he announced his plans and told everyone that he'd signed up to work on a cruise ship." Cameron shook his head, the smile long gone. "What a night. Everyone was crying. Clare. My mother. My grandmother. Uncle John, at least, didn't let a woman's tears stop *him* from doing what he wanted."

Peggi caught Cameron's emphasis. "Someone else did let a woman stop him?"

"Yeah."

He said it flatly, and she feared he wouldn't explain. Curious, she kept him talking. "So what did your uncle actually do?"

"He traveled. For five years. To Europe and Asia, Australia and South America. He did everything you could imagine, from cabin boy to courier. He used to send me postcards with pictures of the different places he'd been. I learned how to read from those postcards. And he would write about the things he'd done, or ideas he had. He wanted to be a millionaire, and when he came back, he knew how he was going to do it. He was going into the computer-chip business."

"Good business to have gone into."

"The timing was perfect. He offered my father a chance to go in with him, but my father—thanks to my mother—said no."

Peggi was beginning to understand. "Your mother wouldn't let him?"

"She cried." Cameron gave a derisive grunt. "Oh, did she cry. Tears always got her what she wanted. She—" He stopped himself, looking down at her, and frowned. "What is it about you? Here I am telling you all about my family."

"It's interesting." It helped her to understand him. "I can see why you admire your uncle. What I don't understand is why your mother wouldn't let your father go into business with him."

"Because she didn't want Dad traveling, going to different cities, probably to different countries. She wanted him close."

And under her thumb, Peggi filled in. "And that's why you don't want to get married? You resent what your mother did?"

"I—" He stopped himself, a frown again crossing his brow. "Ah, I see it now." Raising his hands preacher style, he mocked her. "Woman psychoanalyzes bachelor, saving him from a life of solitude and pleasure."

Smiling cynically, he stepped closer, lifting her chin so she had to look at him. "Are you my soul mate, Peggi Barnett, here to open my eyes to the truth?"

She knew she wasn't going to open his eyes to anything, or save him from a life of solitude and pleasure, no matter what a psychic had said. "No, I don't think I'm your soul mate."

"But there is that hope, isn't there?" His thumb was stroking her jaw, caressing her, his gaze mesmerizing. "That little bit of hope."

"No . . ." She could barely breathe. "No hope."

"Good. Because I wouldn't want you wasting your time. I know I'm never getting married. I, like my uncle, am not letting anyone control my life."

"Slim chance of that. I can't control my own life, much less someone else's."

"Can't you?" Slowly, he trailed a fingertip over her lips, his gaze drifting in that direction, and she shivered but didn't move.

He spoke of control. The one with control was him. He was disturbing her sleep at night, making her want the impossible. He had her confused and frustrated, had her wishing he would kiss her. . . .

Had her hearing bells.

Cameron looked toward the entryway, then dropped his hand and stepped back. Understanding, Peggi sucked in a deep breath and slowly turned to face the two gray-haired women who had just stepped into the shop. They smiled.

"I understand you have antique tea sets," one said. "My sister and I collect them."

"Tea sets." Peggi fought off the fuzzy thoughts that had invaded her mind.

"I'll be leaving," Cameron said, and walked behind the counter to get his jacket. "Oh—" He pulled his checkbook from his inside pocket. "This is why I came over. To pay you for Friday night and your consultation." He tore out an already written check and handed it to her. "Give me a call when you have those designs ready."

EIGHT

Thursday morning Peggi called. Cameron had been waiting. Waiting more anxiously than he liked to admit. At five-fifteen that evening, he stepped into PDQ Interiors.

The bell above the door was still ringing when he heard the first crash. The second came when he was halfway to the kitchen. Cautiously, he pushed open the door, peeking in. A jerk back was all that saved him from being beamed by a flying saucer. It crashed against the door and shattered, joining the other pieces on the floor.

The look on Darlene's face was astonishment. Peggi seemed relieved. "Feel better?" she asked her partner, pointing his way. "You almost killed a client."

The fight gone from her body, Darlene burst into tears. Peggi alone kept her from sagging to the floor. Cameron stepped forward to help, but Peggi shook her head. "I'll be out in a minute," she said.

He decided it would be best to wait in the front. He really didn't deal well with crying women. He remembered his mother's tears, always so close to the surface and easy to flow. She'd manipulated her family with those tears—her husband, her daughters, and her son. Had controlled them all.

And had lost them all.

Ten minutes later Peggi stepped into the presentation area. He closed the issue of *Architectural Digest* he'd been thumbing through and watched her near the table. The blue-and-green colors of her sweater-dress gave a sense of serenity, but the sparks in her eyes warned of trouble.

"Men!" she muttered, and jerked a chair back and sat.

"Problems?" he asked, knowing he was treading on dangerous ground.

She glared at him. "What is it about your sex that makes you such cads? How can one little appendage hanging between your legs turn you into such uncaring, unfeeling creatures?"

He chose to ignore her reference to his possible size. "What happened in there?"

"What happened is Darlene finally opened her eyes. For three years she's hung on to some crazy hope that Jim would grow up, would face the fact that life is not all fun and games, and would come back to her and be the husband she'd thought she'd married. I've told her for the last two years that she should just divorce him and get on with her life, but no, she loved him. And then he does come back, and he tells her he's a changed man, and gets her hopes up. And then he screws her."

Cameron didn't dare grin, not as upset as Peggi was, but her vernacular amused him. "How'd he 'screw her'?"

"By giving her a hard-luck story about a gambling debt. Of course, softhearted, easy-touch Darlene gave him every cent she had left in her bank account. That was Monday, the day you had to fill in for me. Wednesday, she tells me he's gone to settle this debt, then he's coming back for her. She's not sure what to do about our partnership, and asks if I can manage without her for a while. I say sure. Then this afternoon she gets a letter from him. It's a Dear Jane letter. He says thanks for the money, but he's decided she's not his type, and basically, so long, sucker."

"Nice guy."

"A real winner."

"But cads are not limited to the male species." He'd met a few females who would qualify, and had heard tales of horror from his buddies. "My friend Mitch— you met him—had a similar experience. He'd been married two years and thought life was great, then one day he came home and found a Dear John letter. His loving wife had taken off with another man. She'd also maxed out all of their credit cards and had cleaned out their savings account. By the time she was finished with him, he had nothing."

"Maybe you do have the best idea," Peggi said. "Avoid marriage. Forget this 'love and happiness forever after' garbage. It doesn't exist and it doesn't work."

"I'm not going to argue with that." It had been his code for years.

"Just love 'em and leave 'em."

He doubted she meant it, and knew he should keep his mouth shut. Still he found himself asking, "And if I asked you to jump into bed with me?"

She laughed. "The way I feel right now, you might be getting into bed with Lorena Bobbitt."

He winced at the thought. "Considering your present attitude, I'm wondering what my condo might look like if you do decorate it. Will there be a pendulum above my toilet that's activated the moment I unzip my fly?"

"Now there's an idea." She stood and walked over to a file cabinet at the back of the room. "Of course, a guillotine would be a lot faster."

"That would certainly hamper my playboy image."

"I imagine it would."

He watched her pull out a thick folder and an array of samples. She was already hampering his playboy image, whether she realized it or not. Since he'd met her, she'd monopolized his thoughts. She was like so many women he'd known, and yet so different.

"I don't play games," she'd told Edna Miller.

Cameron didn't believe that. All women played games, manipulated men to get what they wanted. Played on a man's weaknesses.

He wouldn't be weak. Not again. Not like his father had been. He wouldn't give in to tears, wouldn't kowtow to a woman. He would see Peggi's ideas for his condo, then he would . . .

What? Cameron wondered. Say no to the deal? Sever all ties with her?

Saturday, he'd thought he'd made up his mind. Today, he wasn't that certain. "If you want to postpone this," he said, "to spend time with your partner, I'd understand."

Peggi glanced his way, but continued gathering materials. "No. Darlene needs time alone. Time to think."

So did he, but it didn't look like he was going to get it.

Her arms filled with books and papers, Peggi returned to the table. She lay out a series of sketches, each fully detailed and painted in watercolors. He could tell she'd spent a lot of time on them. Hours and days. Time she could have spent on other clients.

He felt a twinge of guilt.

"What I've tried to do," she began, sitting beside him, her attitude all business, "is create an atmosphere that's cohesive, elegant, and rational. Something businesslike but comfortable. An atmosphere that lends itself to an afternoon of watching football or an evening of entertaining clients." She smiled at him. "Or entertaining women."

He'd entertained a woman just the night before. He'd called her and made the date Tuesday. After seeing Peggi Monday, he'd felt he needed to go out, needed to get back into the dating game.

The only problem was, going out on a date hadn't helped. She'd been beautiful and she'd been witty, and all through dinner, he'd laughed at her jokes and played the role, but when it came time to either take her home or take her to his place, he'd taken her home. And at her door, he'd said good night. Even when she asked him if he wanted to come in for a nightcap, he'd declined.

There was something wrong with him.

"To begin with . . ." Peggi started, and he leaned forward to look at the drawing she'd pulled out.

She first presented an overall view, then broke it down to a room-by-room discussion. He listened and noticed her perfume, and the scent of her shampoo, and how she made him think of fresh air and sunshine. Even her drawings made him think of energy and light.

Within minutes, he knew he liked what she was showing him. From the basic concept to the individual samples and swatches of wallpapers and fabrics, she'd captured the elegance and the mood he wanted.

At six o'clock, she flipped the sign in the window to Closed and locked the outside door. The phone rang at six-thirty. It was picked up before Peggi had a chance to move, and at seven-thirty Darlene stepped into the room.

"I'm going over to Jim's parents," she said, her eyes red-rimmed and her tone weary. "They feel terrible about what he's done."

"You going to be okay?" Peggi asked, clearly concerned.

"I'll be fine," Darlene said weakly. "I may spend the night there."

Cameron had a feeling she should. The woman certainly didn't resemble the perky pixie who'd cheerfully greeted him a week and a half ago or the fireball who'd thrown a saucer his way.

After Darlene left, Peggi stared at the closed door. Finally, she sighed. "Tonight I understand why you want to avoid marriage."

"You're worried about her, aren't you?"

She glanced his way, and he saw the tears in her eyes. "I wanted her to be happy. She really loved him."

He knew then what a dreamer she was. "Happiness and love don't go together."

"They should. Love shouldn't hurt."

"You're an idealist, Miss Barnett."

"I know, but I keep hoping." Again, she sighed. "Have you ever lived with a woman, Cameron? I don't mean spent the night, but lived—long-term, day in and day out. Really cared for a woman?"

He wasn't sure what she was getting at. "I grew up with three. My mother and my sisters. I cared about them."

"I mean—" She hesitated.

"Mean what?"

"I don't know." With a shrug, she passed it off. "Forget it."

If she had pushed, he wouldn't have told her. He'd told very few. Tonight, though, talking about it seemed right. He needed to talk about it—needed to remember, remind himself what had happened before. "Actually, I did live with a woman, someone I cared for. Her name was Kara. Kara Kaylor. But that was a long time ago. Right after I got out of college."

Immediately, Peggi perked up. "How long did you live with her?"

"A year and a half."

"And you loved her?"

He'd thought he did. She'd taught him how weak that emotion could make a man. As weak as his father. "What is love?"

"Good question, I guess." Peggi smiled wryly. "My experiences prove I certainly don't know. Have you seen this Kara since you broke up?"

"As a matter of fact, yes." It had been a strange experience. "She called me just a few weeks ago. Remember that article about eligible bachelors in the *Tribune?*"

Peggi nodded.

"It was right after that came out." He laughed at the irony of it. "Amazing how being listed as a millionaire will bring them out of the woodwork. She wanted to give it another try."

"But you weren't interested?"

"Not in the least." Which had been a relief. Maybe he didn't need to worry about Peggi. Maybe he had developed the strength he needed. "Actually, I felt a little sorry for her."

"One more falls by the wayside."

He saw it as a stand, not a fall. "It wouldn't have worked."

"You're sure?"

"I'm sure." He looked down at the sketch Peggi had made of his living room. What he wasn't sure about was if he could work with her. Could he stay in control?

"What about that sofa I liked?" he asked.

Peggi accepted the fact that he wasn't going to say anything more about Kara. That he'd said as much as he had surprised her. He was a private person. Part of that control business, she was sure. The less the enemy knew about you, the less they could control you. And she knew he saw her as the enemy.

She was a woman.

Since there was nothing she could do to change that, she shuffled through the catalogs on the table. Besides being a woman, she was a designer of interiors, and she needed to get back to her job. At last, she found the catalog she was looking for and opened it to a marked page. "This sofa?"

It was the one he'd shown her Monday, and he nodded.

"I contacted the distributor," she said. "We're in luck. Barring any labor strikes in Italy, we could get one delivered by the end of November. To do so, however, I will have to order it immediately. Which means you're going to have to decide if you like what I'm presenting here, *and* if the price is right, and let me know in a very short time."

"How short a time?"

"By tomorrow." He looked uneasy with that. "I know I'm rushing you. We're talking a lot of money, and you already know how disastrous a mistake can be. There are other sofas you could get without this rush. Very nice sofas that would certainly do."

"You say this is going to cost me a lot of money?" He glanced back over her sketches. "What's the bottom line?"

She pulled out a sheet of figures and laid it on the table. "Redoing the floors will be your biggest expense, but I think you'll find the oil-finished oak I'm suggesting is money well spent. After that, it depends on the quality of the materials you choose. Except for that sofa, the items I've suggested are high in quality but not necessarily the highest in cost. We could cut corners even more if necessary, but the bottom line for what I've shown you, plus labor and my fees is—"

She pointed to the figure, and he let out a low whistle. "Hal certainly didn't cost that much."

"And look at what you got." She leaned back in her chair and ran her fingers through her hair, pushing it away from her face. "It's your decision, Cameron. As I said, we could cut corners here and there, trim off twenty thousand or so. But if I understand you right, you want an expensive look and money's no problem."

"And you don't get an expensive look for nothing." He glanced at the figures, then at the sketches she'd made. "You're sure you can have all of this done by the second week of December?"

"If nothing major goes wrong, yes."

"And if something major does go wrong?" He looked at her. "I don't want to be entertaining the Investment Club members in a half-finished condo."

She didn't answer right away. She knew this was it. What she said next could make or break this deal. It would be easier on her—on her emotions—if he said no, walked away and out of her life, but she'd put too much work into the project to blow it now. She and Darlene needed this job. Leaning forward, she twirled a lock of her hair between two fingers and studied the cost sheet. What guarantee could she come up with?

Only one idea came to mind. "I'll try to have all of the rooms ready by that date, but I'll concentrate my efforts on the rooms you'll need for entertaining your guests. If I don't have them ready by your party, I'll waive my fee."

"That means you'd be putting in three months for free. Not exactly the way to make money."

"No." She knew that, and she knew she was taking a gamble. "But it also means I'll see to it that those rooms do get done. Remember, with me, money isn't everything. I take pride in a job well done. And if I make a promise, I do my best to keep it."

"So you're offering me a money-back guarantee, is that it?"

"Only regarding my fee. The suppliers will have to be paid. The distributors. I do have a contract drawn up. Why don't you take it home, read it over, and give me a call in the morning?"

Again he looked over the sketches and the cost sheet. Her stomach growled, reminding her that she hadn't had dinner. Embarrassed, she put her hands over her belly, trying to press it into silence.

He glanced her way and grinned. "Okay, I'll give you my decision tomorrow morning. Meanwhile, it sounds like you're hungry, and I know I am. I think this might be a good time for you to pay off that dinner you owe me."

Cameron insisted on taking his car, though Peggi felt it wasn't fair since she was the one who owed the dinner. Once inside his Lexus, she was glad she hadn't subjected him to a Ford Escort, especially one as old as hers. He pulled up in front of the Chop House and handed the keys to the valet, then followed her into the three-story brownstone that had been converted into a restaurant.

Piano music came from the bar, mingling with the sound of people talking. The smell of grilling beef teased her hunger. She'd chosen the Chicago Chop House because Cameron had said he liked steaks, and the restaurant was known for serving some of the best in town. According to its advertising, it was the second-best steak house in America. Not that she knew; she'd never been there. Under normal circumstances, it was beyond her budget, and she'd never ended up there on a date. But these weren't normal circumstances, or a date. Tonight she was both paying back a debt and wooing a potential client.

She'd called and made reservations before they'd left her shop. Seeing the hostess, she stepped forward. "Reservation for Barnett."

The dark-haired woman in her late twenties glanced up from the seating chart and smiled, immediately looking beyond her. "Ah, Cameron. How are you this evening?"

"Fine, Liz. And how are you doing? How's that little boy of yours?"

"Growing like a weed. The two of you together?"

Peggi felt the weight of Cameron's hand on her shoulder, a slight squeeze making the gesture casually familiar and intimately exciting. "We're together," he said, the gravelly sound of his voice bringing a smile to her face in spite of the fact that the hostess was virtually ignoring her.

"You want your usual table?"

"If it's available."

Liz led them up the stairs to the second floor and seated them at an intimate table in a corner. Peggi waited until the woman had left before she spoke. "Liz? Cameron? Your *usual* table?"

"They do serve some of the best steaks in town."

"And you go for the best." She looked around the room, its walls covered with photographs of notable Chicagoans. "Someday I'd like to walk into a restaurant like this and have them say, 'Ah, Peggi, your usual table?' "

"Come often enough and leave big tips, and they will."

She grinned, gazing across the table at him. "And maybe take the hostess out?"

He raised his eyebrows. "Now, is that curiosity or jealousy?"

She knew he had her. "Forget it."

He answered her anyway. "I've never taken her out."

A waiter appeared at their table. "Something to drink?" he asked.

"A glass of Chardonnay," Peggi ordered. Cameron asked for a martini.

As the waiter left, Peggi again glanced around the room. The walls were a dark wood, the lighting subtle, and the atmosphere intimate. She hoped not too intimate. Her anger with men had dissipated from earlier that evening, and sitting across the table from her was one very fascinating man. Every time she thought she'd figured him out, he surprised her.

"That Alice woman came back today," she said. "The one you talked to at my place Monday." She fluttered her lashes. "The one who needed your advice."

Cameron smiled, remembering the woman. "And did she make up her mind?"

"As far as having me look at her living room next Monday, yes. And she did talk me down to a thirty-dollar consultation price."

He shook his head. "I don't know about you." He was beginning to understand why Myra Gibson had said Peggi was too nice for her own good . . . why men had taken advantage of her. "This morning you reduce your consultation fee. Tonight you're willing to do my place for free. That's no way to make money. I think you do need a financial consultant."

"Probably, though I didn't offer to do your place for free. That's just my guarantee it will be finished in time."

He leaned back in his chair, studying her. She interested him. She was pretty, intelligent, and enjoyable to be around. "So tell me, Miss Peggi Barnett, why haven't you gotten married?"

She shrugged. "Because, Mr. Slater, I fall for the wrong kind of man."

"And what kind is that?"

"The strays. The guy who's searching for himself. I

guess I've always had that problem. When I was a kid, I used to bring home stray dogs. Inevitably they'd run off. I just switched from four-legged strays to two-legged strays."

"Ever think you pick up strays because you don't want to get married?"

"Ah." She laughed, pointing a finger at him. "Now who's doing the psychoanalyzing?"

He reached across the table, touching his fingertip to hers. "I'm learning from you."

For a moment she was motionless, her gaze locked with his, then she pulled her hand back, dropping it into her lap. The way her arm moved, he knew she was rubbing her leg. Rubbing off the contact? He also brought his hand to his leg, wishing he could erase the feelings that ran through him every time he touched her. Feelings of excitement and anticipation, of concern and protectiveness.

He took back the thought he'd had earlier in the evening. She *wasn't* like the women he usually dated. In spite of her sophistication, she was too honest, too vulnerable. She didn't know how to play the game, and with a man like him, she could get hurt.

"I want to get married," she said softly.

He immediately tensed. A proposal was not what he'd been looking for. This could get awkward.

"I'd like to have children," she went on. "Yet I don't want to be some man's shadow. I want to use my talents, be my own person."

"Speak your own mind," he added, relaxing as it dawned on him that she was answering his question, not proposing.

She nodded, smiling. "Yes. But it frightens some men."

He could imagine it might.

"Men like you scare me," she added.

Women like her scared him . . . had just scared him. She was the kind who did want to get married. And he didn't want to hurt her. "How do I scare you?"

"You're so sure of yourself." She laughed self-consciously and shook her head, leaning back in her chair. "Listen to me. I'm blabbing my soul out here, and I haven't even had a drink."

"I'm not all that sure of myself," he said. His words surprised him. The admission was not one that came easy for him.

From Peggi's raised eyebrows, he guessed she was surprised too. She only said, "Could have fooled me."

"Cam, is that you?" he heard from across the room.

Glancing to the side, he saw two women at the top of the stairs. He recognized the tall redhead immediately. Jan Caringer was a travel agent, and he'd taken her out a couple of times earlier that year. She'd tried to keep it going, but he hadn't been interested. Up until two weeks ago the thrill of the chase had lost its appeal.

She waved and left the other woman, coming his way. "What a surprise," she said as she neared the table.

Cameron stood and took Jan's hand. "It's been a long time."

He made the necessary introductions, but Jan only gave Peggi a glance. Pretending to read through the menu, Peggi let them talk and silently filled in the blanks.

It was clear that Jan had simply been a quick fling for Cameron. The woman was a good example of what was to come, Peggi knew, if she didn't get her head on straight, if she let herself think of Cameron as anything but a client. She could just see herself one day in the future playing this scene with him. She would walk into a restaurant or a store and spot him across the room with another woman. Awkwardly, they would talk, reminisce over times past, and then go their separate ways.

One day she might sound as pathetic as this woman.

"You'll call?" Jan asked, stepping back from the table as the waiter brought their drinks.

"I'll call," Cameron promised. "Good seeing you again."

"And will you call her?" Peggi asked when they were again alone.

"No." Cameron picked up his drink. "I never should have taken her out in the first place."

"Why's that?"

"Because I just shouldn't have."

"Ever wonder if you'll run out of women?" She shook her head, answering before he had a chance. "Naw. For you, there will always be women."

"You really see me as a Don Juan, don't you?"

"And I suppose you're going to tell me you're not? Don't you worry about AIDS?"

"Of course, but I haven't been going out as much as you seem to think."

"Right." She grinned and sipped her wine. "When was the last time you were out on a date?"

He rolled his eyes and chuckled. "Last night, but I hadn't been out before that for at least four or five months, and I didn't sleep with her."

The thought of him being with another woman stabbed at her, but Peggi managed to keep smiling. "Oh, come on. That's as good as 'I never inhaled.'

Don't forget, I did read that article about you in the paper."

"And don't forget, you can't believe all you read."

"You tried to get me into your bed last Friday night."

"That doesn't count."

His dismissal of the kisses they'd shared hurt. "Thanks loads."

"You know what I mean."

She didn't. She didn't know anything, she decided, and talking about herself made her nervous. She groped for something else to say. "You have two sisters. Any brothers?"

"No. Just the sisters? Why?"

"No reason. Just curious."

"They didn't turn me off marriage, if that's what you're after."

"You told me what turned you off marriage," she said. "You told an entire listening audience, remember? What I'd like to know is what turned you on to becoming a financial consultant. You don't exactly look the type. In fact, if I'd met you on the street, I would have said . . ." She studied him for a moment, then gave her impression. "Sports trainer or maybe a salesman of sporting equipment."

"Sports trainer isn't too far from what I'd planned on being. Although I'd taken business classes, my dream, up until my last year in college, was to play pro football. A tackle by a three-hundred-pound defensive lineman the first game of that season changed my mind. That lardball left me with torn cartilage and the realization that my chances of making the pros were pretty slim. So after I graduated, my uncle used his influence and got me a job at Chicago Fidelity. From there I went into business for myself."

"Uncle John, I assume."

"My one and only uncle." Cameron leaned back in his chair. "By the way, I called him the other night. He hasn't heard from any woman he's dying to marry. Looks like your psychic is a little less than psychic."

"She's not *my psychic*, and I never claimed to believe she was psychic."

"Still." He sat forward again. "There is a chemistry between us."

She would agree with that. She'd felt it the first time she looked up from her samples and saw him. "But some chemicals shouldn't be mixed."

"Too volatile?"

"Absolutely explosive."

"Some explosions are beneficial. They clear the way so you can work without interference." He smiled seductively. "You could call the results *climactic.*"

The way he stressed the word, she understood. She also knew making love with him would only complicate matters. "It wouldn't work."

"You're sure?"

She hesitated a moment, looking at his mouth, then she drew in a deep, reluctant breath. "I'm sure."

Cameron knew he and Peggi viewed life in completely opposite ways. What surprised him was how many topics they discussed over dinner that they actually agreed on, at least in part. He'd never met a woman like Peggi. One moment she was arguing politics, the next she was telling a joke. Well, actually, as she said herself, most politics were a joke.

One thing for certain, he knew where she stood on issues. No trying to read her mind. He liked that. He liked the way she didn't play games.

Her honesty made it easy for him to pay the bill without her knowing. She never suspected he used his trip to the bathroom to cover the charges. Later, the waiter did take her credit card and she did sign a credit slip. She just didn't see the waiter slip the receipt to him.

Why increase her debts when he had money? Besides, he'd enjoyed the two hours he'd spent watching her shop. He'd enjoyed having dinner with her.

They'd lingered over their food for so long, the restaurant was nearly empty by the time they left. Outside, the temperature had dropped, and he saw her shiver as they waited for the valet to bring the Lexus around. "Cold?" he asked, draping an arm across her shoulders and drawing her close to his side.

Peggi knew the casual gesture was no more than a gentlemanly effort to warm her, and she tried to accept it as that. It was her heart that was having trouble staying calm. The moment his body touched hers, it accelerated rapidly, making her light-headed.

"They say we're going to have a cold winter," he said, his voice as level and controlled as usual.

It irritated her that he did have an effect on her after all her lectures to herself and her statements to him that she wasn't interested. There had to be a logical reason for the adrenaline rush. She decided it was the wine. She'd had too much. And it was late. She'd had a long day and was tired.

She was glad to see his car pull up. Once inside, she kept the conversation light, asking him about every button and digital readout she could see on the dash.

By the time they reached her shop, she knew all the finer features of a Lexus LS400.

Cameron pulled into the parking area on the side of the old house. Darlene's car wasn't in the spot next to hers, and there were no lights on inside. "She must have decided to stay over with the Lawrences," Peggi said as she released her seat belt. "I'm glad. I didn't want her to be alone."

"Are you going inside?" he asked, also releasing his belt. "See if she left any messages?"

"No, she's a big girl." And Peggi felt like a little girl, afraid to go into a dark house alone . . . or with Cameron. "You have the contract and that copy of the price sheet?"

He glanced to where the manila envelope she'd given him lay on the backseat. "I have them."

"Then I hope you enjoyed your meal." She chuckled. "Even if you did pay for it yourself."

"You knew?"

"I'm not quite as naive as you think . . . or blind." Resting her hand on the door handle, she realized something. "You're kind of a nice guy, Cameron, whether you want anyone to know it or not. Thanks again for your help Monday afternoon." She opened the door. "I'll expect to hear from you tomorrow morning."

She was running like a scared teenager, but she didn't trust herself with him. Nice guys weren't as easy to ignore as playboys. Nice guys could get under your skin and into your heart.

As soon as she was out of his car, however, she realized fleeing wasn't going to make him go away. Before she had her car door unlocked, he was by her side.

She couldn't just hop in and drive off without saying something, so she faced him.

With the wind still gusting, her hair blew across her face, and she pushed it back, noticing how his hair was being tousled, giving him a wild, untamed look. The light illuminating the parking area turned his eyes a deep, entrancing green, and she realized she should have run. The chemistry was indeed there between them—strong and volatile—and they were standing too close.

Way too close.

"Nice guys wouldn't do this," he said, and touched her shoulders.

She knew he was going to kiss her. She also knew she should stop him.

She didn't.

What she did was reach forward and grasp his jacket. She needed the solid form of his body, something stable. She needed her head examined.

The touch of his lips was warm, the soft, satisfied sound of his sigh a caress. He embraced her, enfolding her in his arms, and she clung to him. The reality of where they were disappeared. Sanity took flight, and she journeyed to a realm of pleasure. Teasing kisses stirred the chemistry, a thrust of his tongue aroused the explosive need.

She tasted the coffee they'd lingered over and wanted more. Hungrily, she moved her lips with his, discovering the taste of passion.

Heated from the inside, she barely noticed when he loosened her coat, slipping a hand between them. Through the knit of her dress, her aching breasts welcomed his touch, the hardened nipples pressing against the confines of her bra and soothed by his caresses.

"You feel so good," he said, nuzzling her neck. "So soft and warm."

"Cameron," she managed, his name a plea. "We've got to stop this."

A trail of kisses brought his lips to her ear. "I can't stop," he said hoarsely. "And I don't think you can either. Invite me in or to your place. Or come to mine. Spend the night with me."

"No," she said on a groan, shaking within. She had to stop.

"We're two adults with needs."

Physical needs. Emotional needs. He would satisfy one, but not the other. "And after tonight?"

"We play it day by day."

She understood. "It wouldn't work. Not for me." She didn't have the energy for another hopeless affair.

"Crazy as it is," he said, "I like you. I really do."

How many women had he told that to? She didn't want to guess. With more strength than she realized she had, she pushed herself back. Shaking, she stared at him. "I need more, Cameron. Love. A long-term commitment. Marriage."

He didn't move. "I can't give you that."

"I know."

NINE

Peggi was hurriedly brushing her teeth when she realized the thumping in the other room was someone knocking on her apartment door. Already late, she swore at the interruption and at herself for not getting out and buying a robe. Once again she turned to the afghan on her sofa.

She called out as she wrapped it around her, "Who's there?"

"Me."

No name. No identification. Yet she knew who it was. Her hand shaking with the memories of the night before, she undid the locks.

"Morning, sunshine," Cameron said, striding past her into the room. "Coffee's here."

He held two Styrofoam cups, and the aroma of hot coffee teased her nose as he passed. The sight of him teased her insides. The envelope clamped under his left armpit, though, dampened any romantic notions. It looked like the one she'd given him.

"I'm ready to sign," he said, heading for her table

and setting the cups down. "But I've had a few changes made."

"Changes?" Certain she needed to be on her toes, she walked over to her bedside table to get her glasses. "What kind of changes?"

"Change changes," he answered. A sly smile curved his mouth when she slipped on her glasses without loosening her hold on the afghan. "You're the only woman I know who can make an afghan look sexy."

"You're the only man I know who comes to my door this early in the morning."

"You said you wanted an answer this morning. You should have come home with me last night. Then you could have slept in. Not that it's that early now."

He was right, of course. The digital clock by her bed said nine-fifteen. Only five minutes ago she'd woken with a start. "I overslept."

"Rough night, huh?"

His grin was too assured, his stance too cocky. She shook her head. "Slept like a baby." A baby with colic, she might have added. Chin high, she walked toward him. "Now, what changes did you make?"

He pulled one of the two copies of the contract from the brown envelope and handed it to her. A quick glance down the first page showed her that just about every paragraph had at least some changes, all very legally worded. "What did you do, call in a lawyer?"

"As a matter of fact, yes." He picked up one of the Styrofoam cups and popped open the lid. "I gave Mitch a call after I got home last night, and he came over."

"After you got home?" She knew that had to have been around eleven o'clock.

"You said you needed an answer this morning. Coffee?" He held the opened cup toward her.

"Thank you." She set the contract on the table so she could take the cup.

Their fingers touched briefly in the transfer, only for a second. But in that moment the skittering awareness that passed through her body reminded her of how intimately he'd touched her the night before. Beneath the afghan, her nipples hardened, and she knew the desires he so easily aroused hadn't lessened with the passing of a night.

Needing the stability of a chair, Peggi quickly sat.

It was time to think, to be alert. Cameron wasn't letting a few kisses and a little fondling get in the way of business. She had to be as detached. "Did you rewrite Hal's contract as much as this?"

"Hal didn't have me sign a contract," Cameron said, and pulled out a chair for himself. "Maybe there should have been one, but we never thought of it. He was a friend, and I was trying to help him out."

"Cameron Slater, Mr. Nice Guy." She was beginning to believe it.

"I wasn't a nice guy last night," he said seriously. "Which brings us to that matter. Ever consider that you may be looking for the impossible? You want love and commitment, something to last forever. But nothing lasts forever, Peggi. People die. Change."

"Grow," she added. "Grow together. How long do relationships usually last with you, Cameron? A week? Two?"

He shrugged. "It was a year and a half with Kara."

"And since then?"

"Since then, I've heeded something my uncle often says, and that is, 'A man can only succeed if he's free to make decisions on his own.' Since Kara, that's the philosophy I've followed."

"By success, you mean monetary?"

He nodded. "I went from owing twenty thousand dollars to where I am now in just ten years."

"And what about emotional success?" Peggi asked. "How are you doing there?"

"Just fine." He gave her a cocky, rakish grin. "Though last night I was devastated by your refusal."

"Oh, I'm sure."

"I do think you're making a mistake by not sleeping with me."

"That so?"

"We'd be good together."

She shook her head. "You have got to have the biggest ego around. Sure you don't want me to leave those mirrors in your bedroom . . . maybe add some more so you can admire yourself from all angles?"

"Only if you want them there when we make love."

"I wouldn't hold my breath, if I were you."

"That's a shame." Cameron leaned back in his chair, still grinning. Teasing her about making love was starting to be fun, even though he wasn't completely teasing. Simply talking with her was fun. One of the reasons he'd come by that morning was because he'd wanted to talk to her, to see her again. He took a long swallow of coffee and watched her.

Seeming uneasy under his gaze, she went back to studying the contract. "You really made a lot of changes. Was it that bad?"

"Not bad, but Mitch felt what you had was a bit too ambiguous. In fact, he said to tell you, if you'd like him to create a standard contract form for you, he'd be glad to do so. That's what he does for a living. He analyzes contracts."

"For a fee, I'm sure."

"He's quite reasonable."

"So are these changes, I guess." She shrugged. "I don't see anything here that I object to."

"I added your guarantee to waive your fee if you didn't finish in time . . . and a bonus of ten percent if you finish before December first."

"You know that I'm going to try to do that." She looked at him. "And you know this is all the more reason to keep our relationship limited to business."

"You should never limit yourself. Success comes from stretching the limits."

"And sometimes failure. If you can't abide by the rules . . ." She pushed the contract back toward him.

"If I can't abide by the rules, you won't play the game, is that it?" He lifted his eyebrows. "Oh that's right, you don't play games. Well, honey, I can ignore a little physical attraction if you can."

"Attractions, especially physical ones, usually fade over time."

"True." He glanced at the contract. "So do we have a deal?"

"It's your call."

He pulled the other copy from the envelope and a pen from the inside pocket of his suit jacket. As he leaned closer to sign the two copies, the sleeve of his jacket brushed against her bare arm.

Fade, Peggi silently prayed. Every breath she took brought the slightly musky scent of his aftershave, the clean aroma of soap and shampoo, and a sense of maleness that captivated and excited her. His clean-shaven jaw begged to be kissed and his wavy hair tempted a touch.

She clutched the afghan tighter and clenched her free hand into a fist. She could resist the physical attraction, what she feared was the emotional pull. It didn't matter if he was nice. He'd made his position on love and marriage perfectly clear. To think he would change was to court heartbreak.

"Your turn," he said, sitting back and handing her the pen.

She signed both copies below his name, her hand shaking slightly. "I'll need a key."

"So soon? I usually wait until the third date."

She ignored his teasing. "I'll need to get into your place to do the work."

"Ah, yes." He reached into a pocket. "I anticipated as much."

He handed her a key ring with two keys. "This one is for the downstairs door from the garage. I've arranged for you to have a parking place for the next three months. Just give the attendant your name."

"I won't be there all the time," she explained. "I'll try to arrange it so I don't disturb you."

Cameron smiled at the idea. She disturbed him every time she moved, her actions fluid and enticing; disturbed him every time she looked at him with those sparkling brown eyes; disturbed him every time she spoke, the edge of her words softened by the melody of her voice. She shouldn't be the one insisting they keep their relationship platonic. It had been his policy for years. Why he wanted something different with her bothered him.

That he'd signed this contract was insane, and earlier that morning—around two A.M.—he'd actually talked himself out of having his place redecorated. It had seemed the best way to go. The safest.

Then he'd reconsidered. Again.

"I'm afraid when they tear up your floors," she said,

oh so businesslike and detached, "it will be an inconvenience. Any entertaining you have planned that I should schedule work around? Clients coming to dinner?" She grinned. "Women spending the night?"

"We'll have to see, won't we?" If she could ignore the attraction, so could he. It would serve her right to find him with another woman. Just because his date Wednesday night had been a flop was no reason not to try with someone else.

Peggi held out her right hand. "Thank you, Cameron. You won't regret your decision to go with PDQ Interiors."

He already regretted his decision. Behind her he could see her bed, the covers pushed back. He might not have been interested in making love with his Wednesday-night date, but the same hadn't been true last night. Peggi's refusal had left him frustrated.

He hadn't slept like a baby; he hadn't slept at all. He didn't believe in soul mates or kismet or fate, but there was something different about Peggi, something special that fascinated and scared him. Her plans for his condo might be exactly what he wanted, but these next three months were not going to be easy on him.

He shook her hand, then picked up his copy of their agreement. The papers stuffed back into the envelope, he rose to his feet. "You'll let me know when to expect workers?"

"I'll be by later today."

A good reason for him to stay away from his condo. "I'll let Pat, my housekeeper, know."

Peggi walked with him to her door. He paused before letting himself out. "I know I sound paranoid, but after what happened with Hal, I do want final approval on everything. You have my office number?"

She nodded.

"Anytime you need to see me, call. If I'm not around, leave a message with my secretary, Mary, and I'll get back as soon as I can."

"I'll do that," she said formally. "And the same in my case. If I'm not at your place or the shop, leave a message on our machine or with Darlene, and I'll get back to you."

It was all set and done. His condo would be redecorated, he would have only a business relationship with her, and everyone would be happy.

Cameron glanced at her mouth and wondered why, if everything was decided, he still wanted to kiss her?

Quickly, he let himself out.

Peggi locked the door after he'd left and leaned against it. She had the job. She would be redecorating Cameron Slater's condo, making a lot of money, and setting herself up to have a very influential reference.

A part of her wanted to shout for joy.

Another part wanted to cry.

How was she going to maintain a "business only" relationship, when the man was already tugging at the strings of her heart?

Soon after he'd signed the contract, Cameron knew why he'd gone out of the country when Hal had been working on his place. Peggi didn't waste any time getting started. Within days, wallpaper was being stripped from the walls and carpeting torn from the floors. When the flooring itself was pulled up, Cameron gave his housekeeper a few days off and he flew to New York City to do some business.

Though Peggi left wallpaper and paint samples for

his approval and they talked briefly over the phone off and on, he didn't actually see her again until the oak flooring was in. He hadn't expected to see her then, but he came home after lunch to pick up some papers, and there she was, standing in the middle of his dining room, giving orders to the paper hangers.

"Floors look good," he said. And so did she. Her black stirrup pants and knee-high boots accentuated the trim lines of her long legs, and the bright yellow vest she wore over a black turtleneck was eye-catching. She'd piled her hair high on her head, but as usual, one strand had come loose and hung near the side of her face.

"I thought you'd like them," she said, coming toward him. "I was going to call you this week."

"Oh, were you?" He said it suggestively, lifting an eyebrow.

She grinned and stopped directly in front of him. "About a couple of light fixtures I found and a bedroom set I think you'd like."

"You're moving right along, aren't you?"

"I have a lot at stake here."

He looked at the stripped walls. "Think you'll be ready in two months?"

"One month, three weeks. I want that bonus." She also looked around. "We'll make it. Darlene's working on the swags for the living room and drapes for your bedroom, and I have those blinds you approved ordered for your office."

"And how is Darlene doing?"

Peggi shrugged. "As well as can be expected. She's started divorce proceedings."

"Think she'd go out on a date? I mentioned her

situation to Mitch. He said they should get together and compare war injuries."

"It might help her," Peggi said. "But I'm not sure she's ready to go out on a date."

"Then it wouldn't have to be a date. Just coffee and conversation. He's a nice guy." He smiled. "Like me."

"In that case, I'll tell her to stay away from him." She lifted her chin. "I noticed you made the papers again."

Cameron knew what she was talking about, and it pleased him that she'd noticed. He'd purposely let the *Tribune*'s photographer take his picture the night of the governor's fund-raiser, the beautiful, head-turning Carbola twins posed on either side of him. The picture had run in the Sunday edition.

"Double your pleasure?" she asked, glancing toward his bedroom.

He smiled. "It was an interesting night."

Her quick pretense of studying an order form said more than words. The idea of him with another woman—women—bothered her. Well good, Cameron thought. Let her be bothered. She'd certainly been bothering him.

Peggi would laugh out loud if she knew just how bored he'd been that night of the fund-raiser. He'd left soon after the photographer snapped his picture with the twins. He'd gone to the party alone, and he'd left alone.

It wasn't other women he wanted to be with or sleep with. It was Peggi Barnett. And that bothered him.

"I don't have the flyers with the bedroom set and lamps with me," she said, starting for the kitchen. "But

I'll stick them in the mail. If they look okay, you can give me a call."

"No."

She stopped and faced him, and he knew he'd surprised her. He'd surprised himself. "I can't tell by a picture if it's going to be what I like." He smiled, a plan taking form, and walked toward her. "I'm a physical man. I want to be able to touch."

Peggi swallowed hard, watching him approach. She'd always considered herself a toucher. At the moment she wanted to draw back and run. For almost a month, she'd avoided any personal contact with Cameron. It hadn't put him out of her mind, but it had helped ease the temptation . . . and the frustration.

She'd actually thought, at one point, that she was getting over the attraction. That was before she opened the Sunday edition of the *Tribune* and saw his picture. That he'd been flanked by two beautiful women hadn't surprised her. That seeing him with them hurt so much, did.

She shouldn't care.

"I want you to take me to some showrooms," he said, stopping in front of her. "I want to see some of these things you're suggesting I put in here."

"In many cases I simply order from a distributor."

"You're saying there are no showrooms, no stores that have displays of these furnishings?"

"Well . . ." She could find places. What she wanted was to avoid spending time with him, getting to know him better.

"Find them," he said with authority, the slightest of smiles touching his mouth. Then he turned away and started for his office.

"Going to showrooms and stores could take a lot of

time," she called after him. "It would take you away from your work, and I know you're a busy man."

He paused at the doorway. "I'll find the time."

He stepped out of her view, leaving her groping for a way out of the situation. "Maybe Darlene could—"

She didn't finish before he was back in the doorway. "Not Darlene. You."

"But—"

"You," he repeated. "Call my secretary and let her know when. I'll tell her to give you priority."

"How nice of you."

He smiled. "I'm a nice guy. Remember?"

She knew he'd won. Crinkling the receipt in her hand into a wad, she swore under her breath. The man hanging paper in the dining room chuckled.

Peggi made the appointment at her convenience, hoping it wouldn't be at Cameron's, and took great pleasure when his secretary, Mary, hesitated. "He has a—" she started to say, then stopped. "How much time will you need?" she asked politely.

"Two hours," Peggi answered. "Maybe more. If this won't work out . . ."

"No, he said to make sure I set it up with you." Mary, as sweet as she sounded, wasn't helping one bit.

Two hours wasn't long enough, Peggi discovered. Cameron stretched the time out until she was ready to scream with frustration. How could she keep up a facade of "strictly business" when every time he touched her, she melted inside, when every minute she spent with him revealed a man she could really like?

She sighed with relief when he finally agreed on a pair of light fixtures, but her relief was short-lived when it came to the bedroom set she'd picked out. "It's nice," he said, stretching out on the king-size bed. "But I need to know how it will feel with two in it."

He patted the space next to him, smiling. She felt like a mouse being lured closer by a cat, and the salesman standing beside her didn't help. "Go ahead," he urged. "He's right. You should see how it will feel when both of you are in the bed."

"Both of us are not going to be in *the bed*," she said, edging back until she bumped into the display behind her.

"You don't like it, then?" Cameron slid off the bed, grinning at the salesman. "Sorry. Looks like we check out something else."

"We are not going to share any bed," she said firmly, irritated that her cheeks were turning red. She didn't need a salesman she might be working with for the next few years thinking she was sleeping with Cameron.

"Oh, I don't know. Let's see about this one." Cameron stepped up beside her, and before she knew what he was doing, he had an arm snaked around her waist and they were falling back on the bed behind her.

She squealed and twisted to get away, only to find herself being rolled over him to the other side. "Cameron Slater!" she yelled, then clamped her mouth shut. Nothing like shouting her situation all over the store.

If she'd ever doubted his strength, he proved those muscles weren't just for looks. He moved her into place by his side as if she weighed nothing, then held her there with barely a touch. Giving in, she stopped fighting. The moment she did, he released her.

"Yep, not bad," he said, and pushed himself off the bed just as easily as he'd tumbled onto it. "My dear?"

He held out his hand to help her off. She glared at him and rolled in the opposite direction. Without a glance back, she headed for the door.

She didn't care what the dumbfounded salesman thought, or what Cameron did. She'd had it. Cameron was playing with her emotions and it wasn't fair. It was all a game to him.

At times she wished she did play games. Then maybe she could roll about on a bed with him and laugh at his suggestive remarks and not have it mean a thing. Maybe then she could be the liberated woman, could sleep with him and not have her emotions get involved.

He followed her, catching up with her before she had a chance to hail a cab. "Come on," he said, and nodded toward his car.

She stood where she was. "I will not be humiliated like that again."

"I was teasing."

"Well, I don't like to be teased. Not like that."

"And how do you like to be teased?"

She faced him squarely. "Cameron, what are you trying to prove?"

The smile left his face, his expression turning serious. "That we need to resolve this, that we can't ignore it." He reached out and touched her cheek. She sucked in a breath.

"You're as tight as a spring whenever I'm around," he said softly. "I trigger something in you, just as you trigger it in me. We need a release."

"And that release is—"

"You know as well as I what it is."

To sleep with him. "I can't."

The intensity of his gaze was riveting. She felt his

frustration, knew his need. She also knew that what would relieve him would only make matters worse for her.

His sigh was deep, then he held out his hand and nodded toward his car. "Let's go look at beds somewhere else."

They continued looking at bedroom suites, especially at beds. Not just that day but for several days thereafter. And then it was dining-room sets, then chairs and tables for his living room. They were scheduled for another shopping trip on a Tuesday afternoon. Cameron was to meet Peggi at the shop and they would go from there. The moment he stepped inside, Darlene pointed toward the kitchen. "She's back there, tending a hurt puppy."

"A puppy?" As far as he knew, neither Darlene nor Peggi owned a dog.

"She found it just a few minutes ago by the back door." Darlene wrinkled her nose. "It's not in very good shape."

Cameron had to agree when he saw the puppy. No bigger than a small house cat, its long golden-brown hair dull, matted, and covered with the blood oozing from a gash on its hip, the puppy looked one step from death.

Peggi held it on her lap, stroking its small head, a telephone receiver in her other hand. She seemed oblivious to the blood and dirt on the front of her turquoise sweater, and Cameron could hear the anxiety in her voice as she spoke into the phone.

"Well, when will he be in? No, that's too long." She looked up at him, but Cameron knew her attention was on what was being said on the other end of the line. "That's all right, I'll find someone else."

She punched the disconnect button and glanced down at the phone book open on the table. "I've got to get this puppy to a vet," she said, punching in numbers even as she spoke. "He's lost a lot of blood and—"

She stopped and said into the telephone, "Dr. McKay's office? I have an injured puppy. . . ."

Cameron listened, his gaze switching between the puppy and Peggi as she explained the situation to the doctor's office. As thin and lethargic as the puppy looked, he really saw little hope for the animal. To take it to a veterinarian seemed a waste of time and money.

"I'll be right over," she said, and hung up. Only then did she give him her full attention. "He'll see us right away. I'm sorry, Cam. I'm going to have to postpone our shopping trip."

All for a puppy who would probably die. He stood where he was, not quite sure what to do. He didn't want to get involved with a dog, not again. He'd sealed that time from his memory. To bring it back would be too painful.

The moment Peggi started to move, the puppy whined and struggled to be free, and Cameron knew what he had to do. "You stay there," he ordered, taking over. "I'll get your coat and then we'll get this puppy to the vet's." He looked around the kitchen. "We need to keep him warm. Do you have a big towel or something to wrap around him?"

"But you don't have to—" she started, then smiled. "There are some in the bathroom."

He got the towel and her coat, and he was the one who carefully wrapped the puppy in the bath towel as Peggi slipped on her coat. Touching the small animal brought back the memories, each as painful as he'd feared, and he quickly handed the puppy back to Peggi. "I'll drive."

"But we'll get your car dirty."

"It can be cleaned." He headed for the side door.

She gave him directions to the veterinarian's office as he helped her into the car. He winced internally when he heard the puppy whimper. The memories were coming—of another puppy's whimper, of a boy's tears.

"I really appreciate this," Peggi said. "I couldn't just leave him."

He glanced down at the animal on her lap. Even covered with the towel, it was shivering. Its deep brown eyes seemed too large for its head, and when it looked at him, Cameron faced away.

"It's okay," he heard her murmur softly. "We're going to get you help, baby."

"It's probably going to die," Cameron said. No need to get attached. No need to care. It only hurt if you cared.

"He's not going to die, not if I can help it."

"He's no more than a skeleton."

Peggi heard the compassion and pain in his voice. His reaction to the situation surprised her. She'd expected him to complain about her canceling their shopping excursion, had expected him to say what she was doing was silly. She hadn't expected his help. "How could someone just drop a puppy off, leave it to starve and fend for itself?"

"People who don't care, who don't want to be bothered by a dog. Jealous people."

His tone was too personal, his voice too full of hurt. "Did you have a dog?"

He kept his gaze focused on the road ahead. "Only for a little while. My uncle gave me one for my tenth birthday."

"And . . . ?" She knew there was more.

Cameron took in a deep breath and glanced down at the puppy in her lap. "He looked a little like this one. Oh, he was fatter, of course. Fat as a butterball." A wistful smile touched his mouth. "And full of energy."

"What did you call him?"

"King. I thought it sounded strong and powerful. He was a golden retriever, and the name would have fit him when he was grown."

"But King didn't grow up?"

He took another deep breath. For a moment she didn't think he would answer, then he spoke. "My mother decided she didn't want a dog in the house . . . or in the backyard. They were messy, she said. But it wasn't that. She didn't want me to have it because my uncle John had given it to me."

Peggi frowned. "I don't understand."

"Neither did I back then. I didn't realize how afraid she was of Uncle John, afraid of the influence he might have on Dad and me." Cameron made a sound of disgust. "She wanted us all under her control, so she cried and had one of her spells, took to her bed for days, and King had to go. They took him away . . . while I was asleep. I never saw him again, but—"

His voice cracked, and she saw his fingers tighten around the steering wheel. She wanted to say something, to touch him, but she kept her hands on the puppy and remained silent, letting Cameron regain control. He was suddenly very human to her, and she wanted to cry for the boy of ten who had had his dog taken away during the night.

He finally finished. "They said they found him a good home."

"I hope they did."

Cameron was glad she didn't say anything more. He'd never come that close to crying, not since breaking up with Kara, and he'd never told anyone except Kara about the puppy he'd loved and then lost.

Kara hadn't understood that it still bothered him. He had a feeling Peggi did.

Once inside the veterinarian's office, Cameron watched how Peggi handled the puppy, how she soothed it and gave it comfort. He listened as she explained to the doctor just how she'd found the animal. He had to leave, however, when her voice broke and tears began sliding down her cheeks. His own emotions were too close to the surface.

Peggi found him at the front desk, making arrangements to pay the bill. She said nothing, simply walked into his arms and pressed her cheek against the front of his coat. He held her close, feeling her sobs and trying not to react. Only when she sighed and looked up at him, her eyes glistening, did he ask, "Did he die?"

"No, at least not yet. Dr. McKay and his assistant are sewing up the wound. He said he didn't know if he would make it or not. The wound's not that bad, it's just that the puppy's so weak."

"He'll make it," Cameron said, giving her a hug. "You're so stubborn, you'll see to it that he does."

She laughed self-consciously, then simply leaned against him. They were that way when Dr. McKay came out. "Our little patient's looking pretty good for all he's been through," he said. "We'll keep him here for twenty-four hours. I'd say, if he makes it through the night, you've got yourselves a puppy."

"So what are you going to do with this puppy if it does survive?" Cameron asked as he drove them back to her shop.

"I don't know," she admitted. "I can't keep pets in my apartment building, and Darlene's allergic to animals." She looked at him.

"Oh, no." He raised a hand. "I don't want him."

"You've paid for him," she said, grinning.

Paid dearly, he would agree, the receipt for the vet bill in his pocket. "Only because I knew you couldn't afford to and that I wasn't going to talk you out of doing this. I can't keep a dog."

"Then I guess the next person to try is my sister. My nephew, Joel, is always asking for a puppy."

Cameron shook his head. "Don't do that to him, Peggi. Don't give him a puppy and then have them take it away."

"I won't give it to him unless Dana and Ted say it's okay," she said. "We don't do things like that in my family."

He slowed his car. "Then let's go ask."

TEN

Dana and Joel were home, and the first thing Cameron noticed was the resemblance between Dana and Peggi. Though Dana was shorter and heavier, and had her blond hair cut short, there was no mistaking that the two were sisters. They even laughed the same way. Joel, on the other hand, had red hair and freckles and the build of a football player, even at the age of eight. Cameron soon discovered that football was one of Joel's passions.

"Mr. Slater played football when he was in college," Peggi told her nephew when she introduced them. "In fact, for a while he thought about going into the pros."

"Really? Who did you play for?" Joel asked, keenly interested.

"Northwestern. The Wildcats."

"My dad took me to one of their games last year," Joel said. "That was neat. My favorite teams are the Miami Hurricanes and Penn State's Nittany Lions, and, of course, the Bears."

"All good teams," Cameron said, remembering

how he'd known every NFL and conference team, their mascots and key players when he was Joel's age. That was when he had the dream. "I almost played for Penn State."

"Really?" Joel's hazel eyes widened. "Why didn't you?"

"I had a mother who didn't want me going that far away."

"Yeah." Joel wrinkled his nose, glancing toward his own mother. "They can be like that. You wanna throw some passes?"

Cameron decided it wasn't a bad idea. His overcoat and suit were already dirty from handling the puppy. A little sweat wouldn't hurt. And while he was tossing a ball to Joel, Peggi could talk to her sister.

Dana waited until her son and Cameron were out of the house before she turned to Peggi. "What a dreamboat." She grinned. "And this is the guy you were ready to throttle in September?"

"I've decided he's not as bad as I thought," Peggi admitted. "But there are times I'd still like to throttle him, and he still doesn't believe in marriage."

Dana laughed. "I don't know about you, sis. How do you hook up with these guys?"

"Just luck." Peggi switched the subject. "The reason we stopped by is I found a puppy this afternoon."

She explained the situation to her sister, including the possibility that the puppy wouldn't survive. "He looks like a retriever mix, so he'll probably be a medium-size dog, but you have the space." She looked out the window where Cameron and Joel were tossing a football, Cameron still wearing his overcoat and Joel in a heavy jacket. "You said once that Joel wants a puppy."

"Ted and I have been talking about getting him one

for Christmas." Dana also watched her son and Cameron. "I don't know. I'll have to talk to Ted first."

"That's why we stopped by, so the two of you could decide before anything was said to Joel. Cameron, especially, didn't want anything said that might get Joel's hopes up if you decide you don't want this puppy. He had a bad experience like that."

"He seems like a nice guy."

Peggi continued watching him. "That's the problem. He is."

They left before Joel's father came home, but Dana said she'd call in the morning and let Peggi know their decision. "What are you going to do if they say no?" Cameron asked her.

"I don't know. Do you know anyone who would want it?"

"No. Your sister's would be a good place," he said, glancing at her. "Joel's a nice kid. He reminds me of myself at his age."

"Really? Wouldn't you say nice kids grow up to be nice guys?" She grinned sassily when Cameron glanced her way. "You sure impressed him, offering to get tickets for a Bears' game . . . on the fifty-yard line, no less."

"No big deal. I have a client who supplies me with four for every home game. In fact, I have four for this Sunday." Again, he looked at her. "I know this is a crazy idea, but Mitch keeps asking me about Darlene. Do you think maybe . . . ?"

He hesitated, and she waited, suspecting she knew what he was going to ask. How to respond was the problem.

He shrugged. "If we went as a foursome, it would give them a chance to meet, get to know each other. If anything develops from there, fine. If not—"

"You're into matchmaking now? You, Mr. Forget-the-Love-and-Marriage-Stuff? Is this the same guy who called that radio show?"

He grumbled and kept his eyes on the road ahead. "I am not into matchmaking. I'm just thinking of your partner. Mitch might be able to help her. He's been there."

"And you just happened to have these tickets."

"Yes." He gave her a piercing look. "You don't believe it?"

She smiled. "Of course I believe it. Why wouldn't I believe you?"

Again he grumbled, but he didn't say anything more. Peggi waited until he'd pulled into the parking area beside the shop and had turned off the engine before she spoke again. "You know, this has been an amazing day. First I expect you to be upset because I have to cancel our shopping expedition. Instead, you take over and drive me to the vet's. Not only that, you pay the bill. Then you drive me to my sister's, play ball with my nephew, and offer him tickets to a Bears' game. Now you're concerned about my partner."

He grunted, looking uneasy. "Look, if you don't like the idea, just—"

"No." She stopped him from going on. "Darlene needs something like this. All she's doing now is licking her wounds and feeling sorry for herself. She needs to get out, meet men. As you said, Mitch might be able to help her, and a football game sounds great."

"Then it's a date?"

❖━━━━━━━❖

"I told you, I don't know exactly how it happened," Peggi said for the hundredth time in the last five days. "We were driving back here, and he suggested the four of us go to this game."

"And you said yes." Darlene stopped pacing the kitchen and faced her. "I don't feel I should be going out on a date. Technically, I'm still a married woman."

"This isn't a date," Peggi insisted, as she had every other time the subject came up. "We are going to a football game with two other people. These people just happen to be men."

"That was a date when I was in high school."

"Well, we're out of high school." And they were playing adult games now.

Peggi knew she was in over her head. Going out with Cameron was not a wise idea. It was bad enough that she was seeing him as much as she was, but those times were connected to the job. This was different.

"He said," she rationalized, "that you and Mitch might have a lot in common. For one thing, Mitch is a lawyer. You might be able to get some tips from him."

"You said he was a contract lawyer."

"Well, lawyers are lawyers. Look, we'll go to the game with them, have a couple of hot dogs, root for the Bears, and then we'll come home. It's no big deal."

Darlene came back to the table and slumped into a chair. "Is that how you feel? I thought you told me you wanted to stay as far away from Cameron as possible."

"And I am." Peggi knew that was the only way she was going to survive with her heart intact. She was getting to like him too much. "We'll put Cameron on one end, Mitch and you in the middle, and me on the other end. I'll be as far away from him as possible."

Darlene grinned. "He still turns you on, doesn't he?"

"He does not turn me on," Peggi lied. "Now, if you don't want to go, say so. But it is a little late." She glanced at her watch. "They should be here any minute."

"I'm nervous," Darlene admitted.

Peggi wanted to say she was too. Instead she faked it. "There's nothing to be nervous about."

The bell above the shop door rang, and Peggi jumped. "It's them," Darlene said, and sucked in a deep breath. "Here goes nothing."

Cameron saw how nervous Darlene was. That didn't surprise him. Even the tension he sensed in Peggi didn't surprise him. He was tense himself.

This wasn't a date. He'd told himself that ever since suggesting the outing. He was simply introducing Mitch to Darlene. That he'd be spending the afternoon with Peggi was merely a matter of expediency. That was all.

He glanced her way and grinned at his reasoning. If that was all it was, why had he spent so much time getting ready, taken so long choosing what to wear? Why did he feel like a schoolboy on his first date with a girl?

She looked wonderful, as usual, dressed in a kaleidoscope of colors, starting with a multicolored winter jacket and moving on down to wine-colored stretch pants and black boots. All during the drive to the stadium, they talked about safe subjects, primarily the puppy. "So your nephew likes him?" Cameron asked.

"Absolutely loves him," Peggi said. "You're not going to believe this, but he named him King."

Cameron lifted his eyebrows, the coincidence too close. "You told him?"

"I mentioned what had happened to you, and Joel liked the name. I think one of these days that dog will look like a King. You should come over and see him. He's already looking better. Once he gets some meat on his bones, he'll be a beauty."

"Considering how he looked the day Peggi found him, that will be a miracle," Darlene said from the backseat.

That Joel was being allowed to keep the dog was the miracle for Cameron. A part of him knew not all families were like his, but another part always expected the worst. He wouldn't be going to see the puppy.

Once out of the car and walking to their seats, they were jostled about in the crowd like bumper cars at a carnival. When Peggi was pushed back against him, her hips rubbing against his, Cameron heard her slight intake of breath. He wasn't surprised. Being so close to her, he hadn't been able to control the arousal she caused. He was sure she could feel how hard he was. That she reacted so strangely to it did surprise him.

At least he was sure that was why she came up with the crazy idea of sitting herself on one end of their foursome and him on the other. He couldn't think of any other reason. He also squelched the idea very quickly, sitting next to her. "I wanted to ask you about that painting hanging in the entryway of your shop," he said to justify his actions.

"The one with all the colors?" She looked surprised.

"I like it. I like the energy it has . . . and the colors. I'd like to buy it, but it doesn't have a price tag."

"You want to buy *Genesis?*" She spoke slowly, then smiled.

"If that's what it's called." He didn't know. "Is there something wrong with that?"

"No." She shook her head, laughing. "Nothing at all. It just surprised me."

"I know I don't have your sense of decor, but I do like that painting. I have from the first time I saw it."

She continued grinning. "I'm glad."

He knew he was missing something here. "So what's the story behind it?"

"No story." She pointed toward the field. "Game's starting."

From the first kickoff, he was back in high school and college, back on the field, planning the plays and working on strategies. In the past, women he'd brought with him had complained that he completely ignored them during a game. He couldn't ignore Peggi. She wouldn't let him.

Her muttering when there was a fumble and her forecasts of the next plays were too much like his. He was used to women spending the entire game wanting to talk about everything but football. A woman who followed the game was a new experience for him, and he told her so.

"It's probably because I went with a football player in college." She laughed. "He was another who decided marriage wasn't for him. In his case, he decided to be a priest."

"Did you sleep with him?"

Immediately, her defenses went up. "I don't think that's any of your business."

"In other words, you did." He grinned, loving how easy she was to read. "You must have been damned good."

She couldn't hide her blush, but she kept her voice challenging. "And why do you say that?"

"It's obvious that after you, the guy decided nothing would ever be as good, so he gave up on sex and became a priest."

"Of course." She laughed at the idea. "And all of the others, well, they were just so overwhelmed by my fantastic lovemaking skills, they also had to take off."

The man seated in front of them looked back. His smile said he'd heard her, and Peggi's cheeks blushed hotter. Edging closer to Cameron, she lowered her voice and whispered into his ear. "That is why I won't sleep with you. I'm only thinking of your welfare."

"I'll take my chances," he said, not bothering to lower his own voice.

He needed some way to end this constant desire he felt for her, and he wasn't worried about being overwhelmed. More than likely, he would discover she was just like the other women he'd known. More than likely, if he made love with her, the chase would be over, and he could get on with his life.

At halftime Peggi and Darlene took off to find the rest rooms. The moment they were away from the men, Darlene grabbed Peggi's arm. "I can't believe it. I'm on a date."

Peggi started to repeat that this afternoon wasn't a date, then clamped her mouth shut. Darlene wasn't objecting. Her blue eyes had a sparkle Peggi hadn't seen for ages. "So you're having a good time?"

"A great time." Darlene actually giggled. "What's not to enjoy? We're with two good-looking men, they're intelligent. . . ." She looked at Peggi. "Mitch is really funny. I can't imagine a contract lawyer being funny, but he says the funniest things. I can't remember when I've laughed this much."

Laughter was what Darlene needed, Peggi told herself, so she had to forget her qualms about being with Cameron. After all, she could resist the man for one football game. Two more hours at most.

"Mitch suggested we go out for pizza afterward," Darlene said. "What do you think? I know you didn't want to sit next to Cameron and you ended up there. If you want to go straight home . . ."

Straight home was the safest course of action, but Peggi knew she had to stay. Darlene was happy. That was what counted. "A pizza sounds great."

"Good. I'll tell Mitch."

They went to Gino's East. When they saw the line, Peggi was ready to forget the idea, but Darlene insisted. Standing next to Cameron, Peggi tried to concentrate on what the others were saying, but her mind kept wandering.

Every minute she spent with Cameron was becoming pure torture. She didn't want to like him, but how could she not? Stereotyping him as a playboy would no longer work, for she now knew the man, knew how kind and sensitive he could be. He was wonderful. Perfect. Just what she wanted in a husband.

Except, he didn't want to get married.

Years ago she would have been sure she could tear down the walls he'd built around his heart, could change his mind. Years ago she still believed in miracles.

Life had taught her different.

"Slater. Party of four," someone called, and they were led to a dark-stained booth in the back, graffiti covering the stucco walls around them.

Peggi slid in behind the table, then scooted over more when Cameron sat beside her. Even so, the sleeve of his sweater touched the sleeve of her sweater, and the slightest of movements brought her leg against his. She sat very still, all too aware of him.

Darlene stopped to check out the writing on the nearby wall. "Some of these are weird," she said, standing on her toes to read one. " 'Kissing frogs is better than kissing dogs'?"

She wrinkled her nose and slid onto the bench across from Peggi. "You're always saying you've got to kiss a lot of frogs before you find your prince, but have you ever tasted that yucky liquid frogs put out when you pick them up?"

"It's not high on my epicurean delights," Mitch said, slipping in beside her. "A pitcher of draft all right with everyone?"

"Sure," Darlene agreed. "Are we going to share a pizza?"

Cameron smiled at the transformation in Darlene in the last few hours. She'd gone from tight-lipped, one-syllable comments to bubbling conversation. Even Mitch had loosened up, telling his usual jokes. The only one who wasn't relaxed was Peggi.

She sat beside him, rigid and silent.

They ordered the pizza and beer, and while they

waited Mitch entertained them with stories, Darlene laughing at all of them. Peggi smiled or chuckled occasionally, but Cameron knew she had her guard up. Finding a way to break it down became his goal. "So what about that painting?" he asked, bringing them back to that. "How much is it going to cost me?"

"How much are you willing to pay?" she asked, playing with the corner of her paper place mat and not looking at him.

Darlene picked up on the question. "What painting?"

"The one in your entryway," Cameron answered.

"Peggi's?" Darlene looked at her and laughed. "And here you were complaining just the other day that no one would even steal that painting."

Peggi continued playing with the place mat. "I guess you can have the painting for a steal."

He touched her arm, wanting her to look at him. "You painted that?"

She did glance his way and shrugged. "My first year in college. My instructor, who also happened to be my adviser, said it looked like there'd been an explosion in a paint factory, that I had an adolescent approach to color that he hoped I would outgrow."

Cameron knew then why he liked the painting. Bright and energetic, it reminded him of Peggi. "And did you outgrow that approach?"

"No, I changed my major." She looked at him, her expression almost sad. "I haven't outgrown a lot of my youthful delusions."

The laughter and conversation continued in Cameron's car as he drove them to Mitch's. Mitch and

Darlene had decided to go dancing. Peggi had declined, as had Cameron, much to her dismay. That meant he'd be driving her—alone—to the shop to pick up her car.

After Mitch and Darlene got out, a heavy silence filled Cameron's car. Peggi looked out the side window, and Cameron searched for something to say. "Did you enjoy yourself?" he finally asked.

"Yes."

"Of course it would have been better if the Bears had won."

"It was a good game," she assured him. "Did you really almost go to Penn State?"

"Where'd you hear that?" It wasn't something he usually told others.

"You mentioned it to Joel."

He'd forgotten that conversation. It had simply come out, the boy reminding him so much of himself. "Yeah. I had a scholarship to Penn State and a scholarship to Northwestern. I picked Northwestern."

"You said your mother made you pick Northwestern, that she didn't want you going far away."

He glared at the reminder. "I'm getting to be a regular blabbermouth around you and your family."

"Did your mother try to control your sisters as much as she controlled you and your father?"

"What is this, another psychoanalysis? Still trying to figure out what turned me off marriage?"

The way he looked at her, Peggi knew she was getting close. Wisdom suggested backing off, but she'd never learned to keep quiet. "Not all of us are like your mother."

"Or so you think."

The bitterness was there, cutting across the car. "Was Kara like your mother?"

"Kara." He made a derisive sound. "She didn't cry to get her way, or have spells, if that's what you mean. But she knew how to manipulate a man. And you want to know something stupid?" He glanced her way. "I let her, just like my father let my mother manipulate him."

He let a woman manipulate him? Peggi thought. The idea astounded her—and explained so much. "So that's why you don't let any get close."

"Ah, she's figured me out." He spoke to the cars on the street ahead. "Dr. Barnett succeeds again."

His laughter was strained, and she noticed his fingers were clenched around the steering wheel, his knuckles white. Peggi knew she hadn't succeeded. All she'd done was gain a glimpse into his past. Nothing he'd told her would change the future.

"I know you're a nice guy," she said, wanting him to understand she wasn't simply prying. "And you'd make a wonderful husband."

He grunted, but said nothing, and she went on. "You play the role of a playboy, but you're not entirely comfortable with that role. You're afraid to have feelings, but you do."

"Says who?"

"Says me." She'd thought about it before, considering all the times he'd helped others. "You're concerned about people. Even that first day, you were late to meet with me because you took the time to help a woman who'd had a stroke. And you set up this date today because you wanted to help Mitch and Darlene."

"Don't go thinking me a saint, Peggi. I spent extra time with Mrs. Weimer because she's a good client. And I only helped Mitch to get him off my back."

Cameron pulled into the parking area next to her shop. The sign on the door said CLOSED, and only two cars were parked in the spaces—Peggi's Escort and Darlene's Chevy. The moment he shut off the engine, he turned toward Peggi. "Okay, you're right, I come from a dysfunctional family."

He laughed at that. What an understatement. "My mother cried to get her way or got all fluttery and weak with these 'spells' she had regularly, and my father always gave in to her. My older sister has been married three times, so far. Have you looked around you? How many families aren't dysfunctional? My uncle has the right idea. The way to live life to the fullest is to stay single. I'm not getting married, Peggi."

"And I'm not asking you to." She reached for the door handle. "Just forget it."

He watched her get out of the car, and knew he should just let her go. Everything that needed to be said had been said. He'd made his position clear.

He opened his door. "We still on for tomorrow?"

She hesitated, obviously surprised. "Tomorrow?"

"To look at more rugs?"

"I'd forgotten."

He came around to her side of the car. Twilight surrounded them, a nearby street lamp adding to the golden glow that fell over the parking area. "Nothing's changed."

Peggi tilted her head back as he came closer, her cheeks taking on a rosy hue and her eyes darkening to a soft umber. "Nothing?"

"Nothing." He touched her shoulders. "I still want you."

"But—"

He didn't let her finish. She had him in an emotional turmoil, and he needed a release. Pulling her close, he imprisoned her in his embrace and silenced her with a kiss, his mouth demanding. Almost punishing. He'd told her too much, had made himself vulnerable. He wanted to take back what he'd given away. He wanted control.

She pushed against his chest, struggling. Her hips rubbing against his excited him, but he knew he had to stop. This wasn't what he wanted, what he'd intended.

As rapidly as he'd grabbed her, he let her go. She staggered back a step, staring at him, confusion filling her eyes. "I'm sorry," he said, angry with himself.

If she slapped his face, he would deserve it. If she refused to work with him anymore, he wouldn't blame her.

What she did took him completely by surprise. Stepping forward again, she placed one hand on his shoulder. With her other hand, she touched his cheek, her fingers soft and caressing. "Now, let's try that again."

He hesitated a moment. "Try . . . ?"

Her smile was golden. "This."

She raised up on her toes and kissed him. Tenderly. Gently. He placed a hand behind her head, this time for stability, not to hold her. She kissed him and he returned her kisses, tasting her and nibbling along the contour of her lips, reacquainting himself with the softness of her mouth.

It wasn't until she pressed her body against his that he embraced her again. The anger gone, he enjoyed what she was giving—her warmth and tenderness, her heart and soul. He kissed her forehead, her cheeks, and her mouth. The dip of his tongue elicited a responsive shiver and a groan from her. Each kiss brought him pleasure—and agony. He wanted more.

"Cameron," she gasped, his name taking on a new urgency when he gave her a chance for a breath.

"Yes?" He tilted her head back so he could kiss her neck.

"We'd better stop."

She said it with a sigh, and he felt her fingers tighten on his jacket. At the base of her throat, he could feel her pulse, strong and throbbing. He was throbbing.

"Peggi, anything that feels this right shouldn't be stopped. I want you . . . to make love with you."

He took her hand and brought it down between his legs. "This is what you do to me. Every time I'm around you, I'm in misery."

She pressed her palm against the hardened length of him, increasing his misery and bringing him pleasure at the same time.

"I want you," he repeated. "It's as simple as that."

She withdrew her hand from his crotch, and pulled back from his grasp, her breathing shaky. "Nothing's simple, Cameron. We shouldn't have gone out today. Shouldn't be doing this. As long as you feel as you do, it's going to lead nowhere."

"Why does it have to lead anywhere? Why can't we just experience it?"

"Because—"

She didn't give him an answer, simply turned toward her car. "Peggi?"

"I can't do it, Cameron," she said, not looking back.

ELEVEN

On Monday, they continued looking at rugs. Neither Cameron nor Peggi brought up what had been discussed Sunday or what had happened in her parking area. Anyone observing them wandering through the displays would have seen only a designer and a client, occasionally consulting each other regarding color and design, exchanging polite conversation, and nothing more.

Peggi, however, felt the strain between them. Being with Cameron was pure torture. She knew he cared for her; she also knew he had not changed his mind about marriage. The enemy was his past, her nemesis his uncle. Cameron's mother had turned her son against women, and John Slater had shown him a life of wealth, pleasure, and freedom. She could not compete.

The rug finally chosen, Cameron and she left the store. They'd driven there separately, and he walked her to her car. "I think," he said, stopping her before she got in, "you know me pretty well now. I'm sure you can pick out the rest of what I need without my presence."

She understood. He'd also felt the strain. "I can always return anything you don't like."

"Then I leave things to your discretion."

She watched him walk to his car. The idea of his no longer joining her on these shopping expeditions was both a relief and a disappointment.

For the weeks to come, Peggi made the decisions alone. Furnishings and accessories were purchased and brought to his condominium. She rarely saw him, and if she did, it was only in passing. It was his housekeeper who let her know Cameron's reactions. Only once did he reject something. It was a painting she brought, a seascape in blues and greens. She'd thought he would like it for his office. He demanded her painting instead, the one from the shop's entryway.

As November came to an end Cameron's condominium took shape. She'd reached the point where all she wanted to do was finish and move on with her life. For two months she'd put other jobs on hold. Now each lamp or picture, vase or plant that she chose brought her closer to his deadline and her freedom from the job. The only possible glitch Peggi could foresee was the sofa. Every time she called the distributor, she received promises.

But promises would not seat guests at a Christmas party.

Finally, they were down to a floor lamp and the sofa. Peggi felt triumphant when she found the right lamp. Its wrought-iron stand was contemporary in design, the smoke-blue tinted glass simple but elegant.

"What do you think?" she asked, holding the lamp out so her and Darlene's part-time helper, Carolyn, could see it.

"Interesting."

Peggi motioned toward the back of the shop. "Darlene in?"

"She's upstairs." Carolyn stepped closer, examining the lamp. "This is for the Slater place?"

"For his living room. If he likes it, I'm basically done. All we're waiting for is the sofa." Peggi started for the kitchen door. "I'm going to show this to Darlene before I take it over."

She found Darlene upstairs in her bedroom, pulling a wool sweater over her head. "I found it," Peggi said, and set the lamp on the floor.

"So you did." Darlene came over and looked at the lamp from all angles. "And it's perfect."

"That's what I thought." Peggi sat on the edge of the bed. In the middle of it was an open tote bag, a silky nightgown lying on top. "Going somewhere for the night?"

Darlene grinned and walked back to her dresser. "Mitch is taking me to Lake Fontana for the weekend," she said, checking her image in the mirror. "I just talked to him. He's taking a shower, then he'll be over. Carolyn's closing tonight and opening tomorrow. You'll be around to close tomorrow afternoon, won't you?"

Peggi hadn't planned on it, but she knew she could. "No problem." Mischievously, she lifted the nightgown out of the bag. "Pretty seductive. So, is tonight the big night?"

Darlene turned toward her, an earring in her hands. "Big night for what?"

"You know. To sleep together."

Darlene grinned, then put the earring post through her lobe. "No, that happened a couple weeks ago."

Peggi put the nightgown back in Darlene's bag. "I didn't realize you two were that serious."

"I'm not sure how serious we are. I just decided I wasn't going to wake up one day ten or twenty years from now and wonder what I'd missed." Her grin grew wider. "And boy, would I have missed a lot."

Peggi laughed, glad to see the sparkle back in Darlene's eyes. "I think he likes you."

"Hope so." She slipped the other earring in. "Mitch says Cameron likes you."

"What Cameron would like is for me to sleep with him."

"You haven't?" Darlene sounded surprised.

"No, I haven't. He's a client. I don't sleep with my clients."

"Meaning after you've finished, watch out, baby?"

"No. Meaning after I've finished with his condo, it's bye bye, baby. The man is not interested in marriage. He's made that very clear."

"So what's marriage got to do with sleeping with him?"

"I don't—" Peggi stopped her excuse. Darlene knew her too well for excuses. "All right, I'm no virgin and I've slept with men I knew weren't going to marry me. But that was different."

"Because you're in love with Cameron?"

"I am not in love with him," she said. "I will not let myself be in love with him. I am through butting my head against a wall."

Darlene grinned again. "Mitch says you've got

Cameron so frustrated, he doesn't know which end is up."

"I haven't seen the guy in a month. How could I have him frustrated?" She was the one who was frustrated. She hadn't had a good night's sleep since meeting him.

"Mitch says you and Cameron belong together, just like that psychic on the radio predicted, but that you're both too stubborn to admit it. I agree with him."

"Well you and Mitch are wrong. Cameron and I do not belong together, I am not his soul mate, and he is not my soul mate. As far as I'm concerned, that psychic can go jump in a lake. And I am not stubborn."

"Right." Darlene kept grinning.

"Yes, I am right." Standing, Peggi picked up the lamp. "Look, I'm going to take this over to Cameron's. You have a good time in Wisconsin. No, have a great time. I'll see you Monday."

"You're taking it over now?"

"Yes. Why? Is there a problem?"

"No." Darlene shook her head but smiled. "No problem."

Peggi knocked on Cameron's door. It was close to four-thirty, after his housekeeper, Pat, left and before he was due home. The condo should be empty, but from the beginning, she'd made it a policy to knock first. When no one answered, she inserted the key and opened the door.

The moment she stepped into his foyer, Peggi knew Cameron was there. His overcoat was thrown over the back of one of the two blue suede easy chairs they'd picked out for his living room; his briefcase sat on the Chinese Amritsar rug that had taken so long to choose. A shiver of excitement played through her, butterflies gathering in her stomach, and she called out his name.

"That you, Peg?" she heard from the other side of his bedroom door.

"I found that lamp I'd been looking for." She hoped the announcement sounded more casual than she felt.

"Good," he called back. "I'll be right out."

She went over to the easy chair that didn't have his overcoat and set the lamp beside it. A few inches away, at the edge of the rug, she found the floor socket she'd had installed and plugged in the lamp. A flick of the switch, and she verified that it was working. Anyone sitting in the chair would have good reading light. For other occasions, the recessed lighting she'd had installed would be sufficient.

When she heard Cameron's bedroom door open, she stepped back so he would get a clear view of the lamp, then she turned to face him.

Her breath caught in her throat, the butterflies in her stomach becoming a solid wad. He walked toward her, a colorfully striped bath towel wrapped around his hips and tucked in at his waist. That was all he was wearing.

"I like," he said, nodding his approval.

The hairs on his chest and head were damp, his jaw cleanly shaved. His tan had faded since September, but he made her think of a barbarian warrior striding toward his conquest.

She forced herself to breath and tried to will her pulse to slow. A month of avoiding him had done nothing to lessen his effect on her. He would always have this effect on her.

"I didn't expect you to be home," she said.

Her voice was whiskey rich, her breathing shallow, and Cameron noticed that other than one brief glance at his hips, she was keeping her gaze glued to his face. They both knew the danger of the situation.

He stopped directly in front of her and smiled. He'd been thinking about her while in the shower. That was the way it had been since he'd met her. No matter where he was, what he was doing, or who he was with, he thought about her. Crazy thoughts. Unwanted thoughts.

"I took off early today," he said. "Met Mitch at the club and worked out, then came home for a shower."

"Well, I, ah . . ." She stepped back, bumping into the back of the chair.

He reached out, catching her by the shoulder. "Don't fall."

"I won't, I mean—" She started to look down, toward his hips, but immediately brought her gaze back up to his face. "I should be going."

She was about to run off like a scared rabbit, and he knew he should let her, but he didn't release his hold on her shoulder. "Heavy date tonight?"

"No, I—" Her gaze went to his mouth.

Only ten minutes ago he'd imagined her in his arms, in his bed. Providence was not something he turned his back on. "I what?" he asked gently, stepping closer.

She licked her lips. "I, ah . . . You're the one who probably has a date . . . or something. I don't want to hold you up."

He chuckled, certain she didn't mean for her words

to be so suggestive. "You are holding me up. Just seeing you gets me up."

"Cameron?"

The soft murmur of his name said she understood; her hesitation gave him hope. He slid his hand into her hair. "I thought not seeing you would help."

"But?"

She was looking deep into his eyes, and he was sure she saw the longing. "I've missed our shopping trips," he confessed. "I've missed you."

She melted toward him, the touch of her hands bringing heat to his arms, the scratchy wool of her coat rubbing against his chest. Her lips were soft and lush, the scent of her sweet and feminine. He wanted to taste and to touch, to explore the emotions she so easily awoke. She reached him on levels he'd never known, carried him beyond the limits of his being to an ecstasy he'd never glimpsed before.

He kissed her, then kissed her again, each kiss becoming more intense. With his tongue, he pillaged her mouth. She sighed, and he drew back. "I want to make love with you, Peggi. You know that. You've known that from the very beginning."

"And after you make love with me?"

He hoped he would have her out of his system, would once again be in control of his destiny. "Do we have to consider that now? Can't we simply give each other the gift of knowledge, the knowing of each other's bodies, the knowing of the pleasure?"

"I don't know."

Peggi fought for sanity, but he kissed her again, another of those wonderful, mind-clouding kisses. She tried to resist the maelstrom of emotions pouring through her, but the effort was futile. His power over her was too strong, the wild pounding of her heart drumming out all reason. Darlene had asked how she would feel ten years from now? Twenty?

"You're not playing fair." She groaned, letting her hands slide around to his sides.

"Nothing's fair in love and war."

"But you don't love me, and this isn't war."

"A war of needs. I need you."

She believed him when his mouth covered hers, his need expressed with an intensity she couldn't deny. And she needed him, she realized. For the moment, for the day. For as long as he allowed. She needed the pleasure he would bring her, both physically and emotionally. To have known him, if only for a short while, would never be something she regretted.

He combed his fingers into her hair, his lips caressing and exploring her mouth. His tongue delved deep, probing and stroking, each thrust an imitation of the act he proposed.

She'd imagined what it would be like making love with him. Alone at night, she'd dreamed of him holding her like this, kissing her and touching her. Possessing her.

In the beginning she'd resisted because she didn't want to get involved in an affair that would go nowhere. She hadn't wanted to fall in love with a man who wouldn't love her back. She'd fought off Cameron's advances with words and denials. Physically, she'd protected herself well. The problem was, she'd forgotten her heart. Somewhere along the way, she'd messed up and fallen in love with him.

He loosened the top button of her coat, and she knew there was no stopping them from the direction in which they were headed. He didn't love her, and when their lovemaking was over, there would be no long-term commitment, no promises. She was also determined there would be no regrets. "Cameron," she said, making up her mind.

"Yes?" he murmured against her lips, loosening another button.

"I need you too."

He lifted his head to look down at her face. She saw the surprise in his eyes and smiled. Reaching up, she touched his face, feeling the smoothness of his freshly shaven jaw and the angles of his cheekbones. Damp, his hair looked browner, longer. She played her fingers through it, aware that he was watching her. "Does that surprise you?"

"No," he said softly, then smiled. "That you admitted it does."

"You're so sure of yourself."

"No. Anything but."

He slipped off her coat, letting it fall to the floor. Next came her sweater, then her camisole. He pulled each over her head, dropping them onto the chair. She turned to let him reach the hooks on her bra. The moment the nylon loosened, he wrapped his arms around her and drew her back against his body, his hands covering her breasts and her bare shoulders resting against his bare chest.

"My living bra," she said, looking down at the large hands covering her. He made her feel small and delicate, sexy and desirable. How she would miss him.

"For the support you want." He rubbed his thumbs over her nipples, each caress triggering a tingle between her legs and sending a shudder through her body.

He kissed her neck, then her shoulders, her bra falling on top of her coat. Then he turned her to face him, his gaze heated and mesmerizing. "So beautiful."

He lowered his head, paying homage first to one breast then the other, trailing little kisses over each and seducing her with the ecstasy of a warm mouth and moist tongue. She purred and she groaned, caught under his spell. Gently, yet hungrily, he sucked a nipple into his mouth, sending waves of pleasure to the core of her.

"I've lost my towel," he said, his words a breathless whisper, and he moved her hands down his sides.

Her palms cupped his hips, her fingers touching nothing but smooth, bare skin. His muscles were taut, toned to perfection from years of working out and the tension of the moment. Slowly, he moved one of her hands closer to the center of his body.

She felt the hard bone of his pelvis and the coarse curly hairs at the apex of his thighs. Anticipation raced through her, her fingertips, her eyes. He guided, and she followed, finding the rigid turgidity of his shaft and the soft skin below.

His eyes were the deep green of a meadow pond, his nostrils flared as he sucked in a breath. He licked his lips, and when she wrapped her hand around the length of him, she saw his mouth part in a gasp.

He was heat and power, all male and virile. Through her fingers, she felt his pulse, rapid and strong. Hers was pounding just as rapidly. She held him in the palm of her hand, yet she was under his command.

"Peggi," he groaned, pressing his mouth against hers.

His kiss was hard and demanding, his tongue a marauder, pillaging and assaulting. It was a blatantly sexual kiss, the message clear, and she responded by sliding her hand along the length of him. Immediately he drew his head back and reached down to stop her. "That will get us into trouble," he said, his breathing ragged. He glanced behind him. "Want to see my bedroom? I've had it redecorated. Lovely woman, my decorator. Good taste."

He leaned close and licked her cheek, then grinned. "Yes, tastes good."

"No more mirrors, I hope," Peggi said, trying to match his levity, though the giddy sensation stealing through her threatened to be her undoing. Fears of inadequacy cried to be listened to, her legs trembling beneath her. She took his hand when he held it out to her, and prayed for strength.

"No more mirrors," he said. "No more handcuffs. No more whips."

"I don't remember any handcuffs or whips," she said, her voice shaky and her stomach muscles tightening as they stepped into the bedroom she'd so recently redecorated.

"I kept them hidden. Along with my inflatable dolls."

She laughed in spite of the tension radiating through her. "You're a nut, Cameron Slater."

The air in the room held the moistness of a recent shower, his bathroom door half-open. The king-size bed she'd helped him choose, not always cooperatively, was covered with a royal-blue velvet comforter, and white and colorfully patterned throw pillows rested against the headboard. He brushed the pillows off with a swipe of his hand and pulled the comforter back to expose the bold blue and white stripes of his sheets.

Cameron's eyes were on Peggi, though, not on the bed.

Her lips were slightly swollen from his kisses, her hair mussed and falling in loose waves of honey over her shoulders, the ends pointing to the milky-white mounds of her breasts. Taut nipples rose from darkened circles. Nipples he'd suckled like a baby and had played with with his tongue.

Women had always been a paradox to him, their softness and warmth to be treasured and pursued, their controlling ways to be avoided. He'd held them at a distance, taking what they had to offer, giving only what was expected. That he'd grown weary of their offerings had worried him. Now he faced a greater concern.

The frightened look in Peggi's eyes tore at his heart. He wanted her as he'd never wanted a woman before, yet the thought of scaring her, hurting her, was stronger. "You okay with this?"

"I'm nervous," she admitted, attempting a smile. "This is a game I'm not used to playing."

"It doesn't have to be a game." Reaching out, he ran his fingers through her hair, brushing it back from her face. "Not if we're honest with each other."

He kissed her forehead, then her cheek. Her neck exposed, he trailed kisses down to her shoulder, then lower, licking her skin until he captured a nipple in his mouth and sucked.

If he were honest, he would admit he was nervous too. He wanted to please her, to bring her the joy she deserved. He relaxed a little when he heard the small sigh of satisfaction that escaped her lips, then relaxed even more when her hands moved to his hair, combing through it and pulling his head closer to her body.

He scattered his kisses, exploring her lips, her ears, and the satiny column of her neck. He wanted her naked, as naked as he was, and loosened the button on her slacks, then pulled down the zipper. Only when he actually began to tug her slacks off did she tense again. "My boots," she reminded him.

He knelt and unlaced the ankle boots, taking off one, then the other. Still on his knees, he pulled her slacks down, bringing her underpants with them. A slight push, and she was sitting on the edge of his bed, and he lifted each foot, stripping her of all clothing.

Finished, he sat back on his heels and looked at her.

For three months he'd dreamed and imagined this moment. He'd pictured her without clothes on, seductively offering herself to him, begging him to make love with her. For three months the tension between them had demanded this moment. Each touch, each look, no matter how innocent, had sparked a desire. In her eyes, he now saw that desire . . . and the nervousness.

He smiled, hoping to reassure her. "Now we're even, both naked."

"No one has the advantage," Peggi said, but knew that wasn't true. Cameron had had the advantage from day one.

She should have known when he walked into the shop and looked at her with those wicked green eyes and smiled that charismatic smile that they would end up this way. She'd changed her plans for him that day. She'd been changing her plans ever since.

He touched her hip, and she looked down to see him smiling. "Love that butterfly."

"It was a whim."

"It's driven me crazy ever since I first saw it."

She frowned, not understanding. "When did you see my butterfly?"

"That morning you were being so self-conscious. When you hiked that afghan up to your chin."

"Oh my gosh." She remembered, and her cheeks grew red. "How much more did you see?"

"Enough to drive me crazy." He leaned forward, arching his shoulders across her hips, and kissed the small tattoo. "You drive me crazy."

His chest was warm against her thighs, hairs tickling a response that threatened to drive her crazy. She could only see the top of his head, and the moment he spread her legs and began a trail of kisses up her inner thigh, she sucked in a breath and closed her eyes. Every little nibble he took, every lick of his tongue sent shivers through her body. She was under siege, his lips moving higher, but she didn't retreat.

Only when he touched her, his fingers brushing over the thatch of hair between her legs, did she open her eyes to find him looking at her face.

Cameron remembered his uncle saying all women were basically the same, especially in a dark room. Until today, he'd agreed. Over the years he'd known many, one not much different from the next. They'd come and they'd gone, satisfying a physical need but little more.

Today, he was glad the room was light. Today he wanted to see Peggi, see the soft, curly honey-colored hairs that guarded her womanhood, see the flush of color in her cheeks. She was a mystery, one he wanted to explore.

The scent of her was sweet and alluring, her responses to his touch swift and satisfying. Almost imperceptibly she spread her legs farther, inviting him to go on. He accepted the invitation, a kiss and a touch bringing his name to her lips.

"Cameron," she gasped, putting her hands on his head to stop him. "I—"

She didn't finish, and he didn't stop. Heat radiated from her body, small moans expressing her desires, the writhing of her hips goading him on. She was moist and swollen and on the edge. Too far, and he would lose her.

Rising to his feet, he opened the nightstand that matched the bed and pulled out a foil packet. It took him only a minute, then he was leaning over her, his hands spanning her sides, his knees spreading her thighs. "Peggi, look at me."

She did, and he knew he would never forget this moment. Passion darkened her eyes to a steamy cocoa, her lambent gaze embracing him. "I've wanted this for so long," he confessed, amazed it was really happening. "Both of us have wanted this."

He laid her down and slowly, carefully, he penetrated her. Peggi knew he was right. She had wanted this as much as he had. Her protests had been futile, her denials a sham. Looking up, she wished she hadn't removed the mirrors above his bed, that she could see the union of their bodies. Never before had she wanted to look. Never before had it felt so perfect.

She wrapped her legs around him and held him close, feeling the sweat build on his body, the cording of his muscles. He was a part of her, inside of her and surrounding her, and she was a part of him. He took her breath away and he gave her life. Deeper and deeper he filled her, pushing her beyond sanity.

Her entire body convulsed when her release came. He followed, using her rhythms as his own. It was volatile. Explosive. Everything they had known it would be. And then he relaxed against her, his sigh one of exhausted pleasure. "I was right," he said near her ear.

"About what?" Not that she cared. She was too emotionally drained to care.

"That we'd be good together." Tenderly, he kissed her lips.

Peggi closed her eyes, wishing he'd said nothing. She was a conquest, another in his lineup. She'd accepted the terms before stepping into this room, yet a small part of her had hoped . . . had dreamed.

"Give me a minute," he said, pushing himself off her. "I'll be right back."

He went into the bathroom, and she sat up, hooking her heels on the edge of the mattress and drawing her knees to her chin. Arms wrapped around her legs, she knew she was shielding herself. Reality made her vulnerable.

She'd made love with him. She'd given herself to him completely.

She loved him.

And it didn't make a damned bit of difference.

TWELVE

Cameron came out of the bathroom and saw Peggi sitting on the edge of his bed, her knees drawn up to her chin, her legs protecting her body from view. Eyes closed, she didn't move, and he stood and stared at her.

Something had happened, when they'd made love. Something deep and soul shattering, and he wasn't quite sure how to deal with it.

Peggi had touched him. Not just physically, but emotionally. She'd fulfilled him in ways that went beyond sex. In her honesty, she'd forced him to shed his pretenses, had forced him to feel and experience with his heart, not just his body. What they'd shared was unlike anything he'd known before, and it frightened him.

He'd expected the act of making love to ease the tensions and cleanse her from his system. It hadn't happened. Though he was physically satiated, the feelings were still there, the desire to touch her and hold her close as strong as before.

He walked over and sat beside her, slipping an arm around her shoulders. "You okay?"

"Sure." She smiled, but he saw the glistening of tears in her eyes.

"Don't cry." It brought back too many memories. "I hate crying."

"I'm sorry." A swipe at her eyes with the back of her hand rubbed away the tears. "I don't know why I am crying." She tried a laugh. "You weren't that bad, really."

He knew then that their lovemaking had touched her as deeply as it had him and that she didn't know how to deal with it any more than he did. Laughter, perhaps, was the best way. "Now aren't you glad you didn't install that guillotine?"

Giving her shoulders a squeeze, he brought them to their feet. "I need another shower. How about you? Then we can see what Pat left me for dinner. She always cooks enough for two."

Peggi knew making love with Cameron had been a mistake. Darlene had been wrong. Waking up ten or twenty years from now wondering what she'd missed wouldn't have been half as bad as knowing what could have been.

Three months ago Peggi had laughed at the idea of Cameron being her soul mate. Now she knew that psychic had been right, at least for her. Never in her life had she felt so complete. Never before had making love been such an earth-shattering experience.

If only he felt the same way.

Sharing a shower with Cameron, his large hands spreading a lather of soap over her back, a spray of water hitting her face, she wondered what he was feeling. To him, was she simply one of many? The evening's catch?

She turned to face him. "Is this your usual procedure, Mr. Slater? You make love with the woman, then you bathe her?"

A dark scowl immediately creased his forehead. "Make love with *the woman?*"

"You know what I mean. Your reputation precedes you."

"My reputation as a playboy?" He half laughed. "I know you're not going to believe this, but I haven't been with a woman for over six months."

She wanted to believe him, and yet . . . "The Carbola twins?"

He shrugged. "Were at a party I attended. We had our picture taken together. That was all." He brushed her wet hair back from her face. "Now you know the truth. I'm a phony."

He gave her nose a tweak, then pushed back the shower door. "I'll find us something to wear while you finish up."

His quick escape told her more than words. For a moment he'd opened up to her and now his guard was again in place. She had gotten a step closer . . . and that had scared him.

He was smiling when she stepped out of the shower. Clothed in a blue terrycloth robe himself, he held in his arms a cranberry-colored robe made of soft velour. "I looked all over for an afghan, but this was the best I could find."

She grinned, remembering the times he'd dropped by her apartment unexpected. "It will do."

"I suppose I could give it to you without the sash. That might make it as tantalizing as that afghan."

"I never meant to tantalize you."

"Oh, I'm sure."

"Really."

He didn't argue, simply handed her the robe and retreated.

Peggi found him in the kitchen, warming the chicken his housekeeper had prepared. She'd been thinking as she'd dried her hair. Once again she'd fallen in love with a man who had vowed never to marry. She hadn't learned a thing from past experiences; only this time, she feared, the ending was going to be worse than before.

After his departure, Craig had rapidly lost his hold on her heart. The others were faint memories. It wasn't going to be as easy to forget Cameron. Over the last three months he'd become a part of her, growing on her without her even realizing it. Once, she'd thought their verbal sparring matches were irritating. Now she knew she was going to miss them. Another week or two and their connection would be over, his sofa, she hoped, would be delivered, and her part of the contract would be fulfilled. His condominium would be refurbished, and he would put on his party.

A part of her wanted to hope that Cameron loved her, that things would be different this time, but she knew that was wishful thinking. "You've only lived with one woman?" she asked, leaning against the counter and watching him.

He glanced her way before sticking two potatoes into the microwave, and she knew her question had taken him by surprise. "Yes. Why?"

"Just curious." And foolish, she knew. Learning

about his past wasn't going to change anything. "Want me to make a salad?"

"Sure." Cameron watched her go to his refrigerator. He knew what she wanted to ask . . . would he consider living with her? He'd thought about it. Briefly. Just as quickly he'd known it wouldn't work.

"Let me tell you what happened with Kara," he said, hoping to explain. "The problem with us was, I loved her too much. I became the slave; she the master. She snapped her fingers, I jumped."

Peggi closed the refrigerator door, a head of lettuce in one hand, a tomato in the other. She didn't move, simply looked at him, and he went on. "I'd vowed I would never be like my father, would never let a woman run my life, but there I was, doing exactly the same things he had done. I had a chance at a job in New York City. I would have been right there on Wall Street. Kara didn't want me to go."

"So you turned it down?" Peggi asked, walking toward him.

He snorted in disgust with himself. "She cried and said if I loved her I wouldn't take the job. It was the same act my mother always used on my father, and fool that I was, I gave in, just as he always gave in to my mother. My father's weakness ended up killing him. In my case, two months later, Kara said there was this guy she'd met at work and—" The memory still angered him. "And that was the end of love and forever after."

Peggi laid the lettuce and tomato on the counter and touched his arm. "That happens when one person is in love and the other one isn't, it—"

He stopped her. "No, it happens when a person doesn't learn from the past. I'm slow, but I do learn." He chuckled. "You know what I liked? When she called me a few months ago. It was a nice feeling, saying, 'Don't call me, I'll call you.' And it was ironic. If she hadn't dumped me, I probably never would have taken my uncle's advice and gone into business for myself, wouldn't have made the money I've made, and never would have had my name in the paper. Like my father, I would have worked my tail off at a go-nowhere job until it killed me."

"And now you have everything you want."

He hesitated before answering. Three months ago he would have immediately said yes. Three months ago his work had seemed enough. Looking at Peggi, looking deep into her eyes, he was no longer sure of that, but to admit anything else would be too dangerous. "I have everything I want," he lied smoothly, and turned away. "I think I'll open some wine."

While Peggi put together the salad Cameron opened a bottle of Chardonnay and brought down two glasses. She dished the food onto plates, and he grabbed a beach towel from the linen closet and waved her into the living room.

The towel became a tablecloth, the floor near the windows their table. Two candles illuminated the scene, and they sat cross-legged on the floor, Lake Michigan and a star-studded sky in front of them. The soft music coming from his sound system surrounded them. "To tonight," he toasted, tapping his wineglass against hers.

"To tonight," Peggi repeated, knowing she would never forget this night . . . or Cameron. A tear slipped down her cheek, and she looked away.

She wouldn't cry, not in front of him. He'd explained his position from the very beginning. That he hadn't changed wasn't his fault. She was the one who hadn't learned.

"Have you been downtown to see the Christmas decorations?" he asked, setting a chicken leg back on his plate and wiping his hands on a paper towel.

Casual conversation had been the norm since Cameron had gone to get the wine. It was safer, Peggi knew. She held up her part. "I took Joel to the Christmas-tree lighting at Daley Center." She laughed and grabbed a paper towel for herself. "He wanted to bring King along. I had a heck of a time explaining that a four- or five-month-old puppy wouldn't be welcomed."

"The dog's still doing okay?"

"Growing by leaps and bounds. You should come see him sometime."

"I will."

She knew he wouldn't.

Cameron looked around his living room. Peggi's touch was everywhere. "Pat wants to put up some Christmas decorations. I told her to talk to you."

"She did. Monday she's going to show me what you have."

"Whatever you think is needed, go ahead and buy it. I want a festive mood for that party. You're sure the sofa will be here in time?"

He stretched back, lying on the floor space that should have been covered by an eight-foot cream-colored leather sofa. Its absence gave the room a barren look.

"I called again this morning. They promised delivery in ten days." She held up her crossed fingers.

He'd told himself when he got out of the shower

that it would be a mistake to make love with her again. In the kitchen, their conversation about Kara had reinforced his feelings that letting his relationship with Peggi go any further would be disastrous. But looking at her, her lips shiny with the grease from the chicken, her hair falling softly over the folds of his robe, he knew he wanted her again, foolish or not.

"No sofa, no money," he warned, twisting to the side and grabbing the back of her robe.

With a jerk, he pulled her to him, catching her before she hit the floor. She squealed and rolled over, straddling his legs. "You wouldn't dare, Cameron Slater. You're the one who wanted that imported Italian leather sofa."

"You're the one who signed that contract."

"But—"

"This butt?" he asked, catching his hands under her behind and lifting her so she fell onto his chest.

He was laughing when he kissed her.

They made love again. On the oiled-oak flooring, his robes became their mattress, precautions only remembered at the very last minute. After they made love, they finished their dinner and talked and drank wine until the bottle was empty, the hour was late, and the need to make love with Peggi again ruled stronger than Cameron's common sense.

This time he carried her to his bed and laid her in the center. There he took his time, savoring every minute and making certain her needs were met before he satisfied his own. It wasn't until she was snuggled against the curve of his body, her breathing the soft rhythm of sleep, that he considered what he had done.

He'd meant their lovemaking to be a onetime experience, a release of the frustrations and a satisfaction of his curiosity. He was finding his appetite for her insatiable, each release only making him want more. The dilemma was troubling. If one night was not enough, how many would be? Two? Three? A thousand?

A long-term commitment was out of the question. Commitment, he'd learned, meant a loss of control. He needed to think this out, needed to do something.

His thoughts were a jumble.

Closing his eyes, he inhaled the sweet, womanly smell of Peggi. Perhaps, in the morning, he would see things clearer. Or, perhaps, he might just make love to her again.

Cameron hadn't drawn the heavy drapes that Darlene had created for his bedroom windows, and the room was filled with light when he opened his eyes to find Peggi lying on her side, looking at him. "Morning," he said, stretching his arms and legs.

"Morning." She smiled and reached out to touch his chest.

Her hand was small and warm, her touch the stimulus for reaction. The need was still there. He brushed the tangled locks of her hair back from her face, marveling at how silky they still felt. "How are you?"

"Good." Her smile grew wider. "Great."

He touched her hip. "And down here?"

"Not bad. Stiff." She moved her legs, arching her back. Her hips bumped against his. "Speaking of stiff . . ." Her smile became sensual. "I notice you're in full form."

"You have this effect on me."

"So you once said."

"Getting tired of it?"

"Never."

"Interested?" He rubbed his hips against hers.

"Do cats like catnip?"

"This cat's about to nip."

Peggi didn't see how it could get any better than it had been the night before, but when Cameron began nibbling at her neck, she knew she was in for a few more surprises. She didn't consider herself a novice in the field of lovemaking, but she'd never met a man who paid as much attention to her needs while satisfying his own.

He tried different positions, prolonging the ecstasy and heightening her pleasure. He touched her in different ways, slowly driving her crazy while she was loving it. He was serious and he was playful, and she knew she would never love anyone as she loved him.

I love you, she thought, those three words playing over and over in her mind. He quickened his rhythm, and she gripped his shoulders. Breathing became impossible, her body tensed. Every nerve ending was ready, every thrust carrying her closer.

Closer.

Her release was sudden, the ricocheting sensations easing the tension and the waves of pleasure buffeting her emotions. *I love you* once again played through her head.

She didn't realize she'd said the words aloud until Cameron's body grew rigid. He couldn't stop the pulsing deep within her, but his torso didn't move, his gaze riveted on her face. She knew what was wrong and decided not to deny it.

"I love you," she repeated, sounding far calmer than she felt.

"Peggi." He pulled away from her, the few inches between them as wide as a chasm.

"I know what you're going to say." She wanted it to be different, but had no delusions.

"I just—" He hesitated.

"Don't want to repeat the past?" She sat up, drawing the sheet with her as she did. "Cameron, I'm not your mother. Or Kara. I'm me. Peggi Marie Barnett."

"It doesn't matter who you are." He voice was cool. Sitting, he didn't look at her.

"So now you're going to run?"

"Don't be silly." He pushed himself out of bed and grabbed for his robe.

"Am I being silly?" She didn't think so. "What would you call it if not running?"

"Being—" he started, then stopped with a disgruntled sound. "If I'm running, it's because I want to be free. I will not be controlled by a woman. Never again."

"I don't want to control you. That's not what love's about."

"Isn't it?" He faced her. The tenderness she'd seen earlier was gone, his eyes now an icy green.

"Love is caring for another person," she said. "Wanting what's best for that person. Kara didn't love you when she stopped you from going to New York City. If she had loved you, she wouldn't have left you so soon after that. Cameron, I wouldn't know how to control you if I could."

He laughed sarcastically. "All women know how. You're born with ways. Tears. Your ability to play helpless. Threats."

"Have I cried, played helpless, or made any threats?"

"Not yet, but one day . . ."

"I might cry. Yes. I cry because I have emotions. Because I allow myself to feel emotions. And I might be helpless. I'm not invincible. But I don't make threats. You do."

"I've learned it's better to take the position of strength."

"No, what you're taking is the easy way out."

"I'm taking the smart way. My uncle has always had the right idea. Stay footloose, make money, and be happy."

"And how do you know he's happy?"

"I know."

"So you close yourself off to all emotion, use women for sexual gratification, then dump them?"

"I'm not dumping you."

"Oh yeah? What are you doing, Cameron? What is our future?"

He stared at her for a moment, then turned away. "We'll talk about this later. I'm going to take a shower. Then I'll fix us some breakfast."

She didn't say anything, but she was dressed and out of his condo before he finished his shower.

She held back the tears until the elevator doors closed, then they came, streaming down her cheeks. On the fifth floor, the elevator stopped and a young couple with a baby got on. Quickly, Peggi wiped her eyes and ran her fingers through her hair, trying to give it some semblance of order.

Her coat buttoned over clothes that had been thrown on, her bra and camisole stuffed in her purse, she felt like a call girl. Both the husband and wife glanced her way, then stepped to the opposite side of the elevator. The doors closed and they began talking to their baby.

Peggi might have thought they were ignoring her if the mirrors lining the elevator's walls hadn't shown how many times they glanced at her reflection, then at each other. Their looks were pitying, and all she could hope was that she never saw them again. She didn't want pity. She'd been the stupid fool. She deserved to be miserable.

He'd warned her. She'd known from the very beginning that he was afraid to love. She'd told herself she'd learned from the past, that she was through trying to mend wounded psyches. Where she'd gone wrong, she didn't know.

She shouldn't have spent so much time with him, shouldn't have joined him on all those shopping trips. She'd deluded herself thinking she could handle it. All the while, she'd been falling under his spell.

The elevator doors opened at the lobby and the couple with the baby stepped out. Another floor down and she was at the garage. Only when she was in her car, driving to her apartment, did she voice her anger. "Damn you, Cameron Slater!" she said to the cars on the road in front of her. "How can a man who acts so loving be so cruel?"

He knew she was gone the minute he stepped out of his bathroom. He wasn't surprised. He also knew he'd hurt her.

"I warned her," he said to the empty room, his gaze locked on his bed, the two pillows side by side re-

minding him of how he'd been with Peggi such a short
time before.

He hadn't meant to hurt her. Dammit all, he liked
her. Liked the way she sashayed into a room. Liked her
smiles, and the way she got all serious when pondering
a question. He liked arguing with her—and laughing.

Liked making love with her.

"Damn!" he swore, and strode over to his dresser.
He wouldn't think about it. Sure he would miss
her . . . for maybe a day or two. She was different
from the others. He'd let her get closer, but he would
get over her.

He threw on a sweatshirt and jeans, not bothering
with shoes. He needed a cup of coffee to clear his
mind.

The moment he stepped out of his bedroom, he
saw the glasses and plates on the towel in front of the
living-room windows. The empty bottle of wine was on
its side, his cranberry robe lying on the floor. It drew
him to it.

He picked up the robe and buried his face in the
soft velour, the texture reminding him of the feel of
Peggi's skin, her scent now a part of the material. Eyes
closed, he remembered, images playing through his
mind. Her smiling up at him . . . his brushing a lock
of hair back from her face . . . them laughing . . .
her sighing. He'd kissed away that sigh and had turned
her laughter into purrs of delight. He'd made love to
her to banish her from his thoughts.

Now she was seared into his memory.

He dropped the robe and walked away from the
dishes. It was over. Done. Finished. A couple of more
weeks and she would be finished with the redecorating
of his condo and completely out of his life. He would

forget her, banish her to the far recesses of his mind. He would go on with his life as he had it planned.

Nothing had changed.

Less than a week later Cameron knew things had changed. He realized it when he stepped into his condominium and saw Darlene helping Pat decorate his Christmas tree. "Where's Peggi?" he demanded.

Darlene didn't flinch. "She asked me to take over. She's busy on another job."

"We have a contract."

"Which will be fulfilled. There's only a little left to be done here. Your tree will be decorated today, and the sofa should be here next Monday or Tuesday."

Cameron walked away, slamming his briefcase down on the desk in his office. He didn't envy Mitch. As tiny as Darlene was, she was one stubborn woman.

And so was Peggi.

Stubborn and manipulative. She could say she wasn't like Kara, but she was. She'd avoided him since Saturday—now this. If she thought staying away would change his mind, she was wrong. He wasn't going to go crawling to her, begging her to come back, just to be rejected. And it didn't matter that his housekeeper was telling him he was a fool. He was in control.

"I'm flying down to Bermuda," he announced, stepping back out of his office.

Both Pat and Darlene stopped decorating the artificial tree in the corner of the living room and stared at him. "What about the party?" Pat asked.

"I'll be back by then. You have everything set up, don't you? The caterers, the bartender, and the musicians?"

"Everything's set up and ready," she confirmed. Darlene was smiling.

"What's so funny?" he asked her.

"Nothing." She didn't stop smiling, though. "Is this trip to Bermuda for business or are you escaping"— she paused meaningfully "—the city for a while?"

"I'm visiting my uncle." He needed a reality check.

"Ah . . . your uncle John."

That she knew so much about him irritated Cameron. That he wanted to ask her how Peggi was, irritated him more. "I expect this place to be ready when I return, and that means the sofa in place."

"I'm sure you'll find everything to your satisfaction."

Nothing was to his satisfaction. Not Darlene's smug grin, not the way he'd been tossing and turning for the last five nights, not even his date the evening before. Going out to dinner with other women was not helping him get Peggi out of his system.

He needed to talk to his uncle.

"He's gone where?" Peggi asked.

"To Bermuda. To see his uncle." Darlene sat in the kitchen chair opposite Peggi. "He didn't look like he'd been sleeping well."

"So he's going down there to get some sleep?"

"That's not what he said. He called it a visit. I think he's trying to get away from you."

Peggi frowned. "I haven't been bothering him."

Darlene grinned and leaned back. "I think you have been. Pat said he's been an absolute bear the last few days, that he snaps at her, doesn't finish the dinners she leaves. I think you've been bothering Mr. Cameron Slater very much."

"Well in that case, good. He deserves it." She certainly hadn't spent a very enjoyable week since her departure from his condominium. "Not that I have any hopes that anything is going to change. That's why he's going down to see his uncle. The two of them will get together and share stories about the wonders of being bachelors. He'll probably be partying all the time he's down there."

While she sat around being miserable.

"I've got to get out of here."

Cameron paid the cabdriver, then walked up the stone steps to his uncle's villa. At the top of the stairs, he paused, staring out at the dark body of water that formed his uncle's backyard. Above, a three-quarter moon illuminated the sky, reflecting off the ebbing tide and painting the shoreline a peaceful calm.

Over the last ten years Cameron had come to this house many times. Always he'd found the direction he needed. The lessons he'd learned from John Slater had been simple: Be honest in your dealings with others, make things happen, and don't let a woman stop you from following your dreams.

John had followed his dreams. He'd traveled, had made things happen, and was respected as an honest man. Now he had houses in Menlo Park, California; Sydney, Australia; and Bermuda. What better place to live than Bermuda? Cameron asked himself. Especially in December.

The overcoat he'd worn to O'Hare had long ago been removed, and his wool suit was uncomfortable in the tropical temperature. In the tote bag he carried were shorts, polo shirts, and sneakers. That would be his wardrobe for the next few days.

"Ah, Mr. Cameron," the man who answered the door said. "Mr. Slater is expecting you. He's on the deck."

Cameron left his tote bag in the hallway and went to his uncle. John smiled the moment he saw him, extended a hand, then changed his mind and hugged him. "How are you, my boy?"

"Not bad," Cameron lied.

"You can't imagine how surprised I was to get your call this morning. I've been meaning to call you. I've just been so busy lately."

He motioned Cameron over to the railing and pointed down the shoreline where a woman was walking along the water's edge, the moonlight turning her into a silhouette. "Remember that call you made to me two or three months ago? When you asked if any woman had called who'd made me change my mind about marriage?"

John grinned like a Cheshire cat. "Well, three weeks ago, a woman did call—a woman from my past. Do you remember Clare?" He shrugged, still grinning. "You probably don't. You were only four years old the last time you saw her. But back then, you thought the world of her."

"Clare?" Cameron did remember. "The girl who baby-sat me? Your high-school girlfriend?"

His uncle nodded. "She called me . . . and I did change my mind. Congratulate me, Cameron. I'm getting married."

THIRTEEN

Tuesday afternoon, Darlene called Peggi. "The sofa was delivered this morning," she said. "I watched them deliver it, just like you said to do, and everything looked fine. No cuts. No marks on the leather. As far as I could tell, it's exactly what was ordered."

"So what's the matter?" Peggi asked. Darlene's tone was unmistakably worried.

"He called me just five minutes ago and said—"

"He?" Peggi interrupted.

"Cameron."

"I thought he was in Bermuda."

"He was. He's back. And not in the best of moods, either."

"What makes you say that?"

"Because," Darlene went on, "he said he would not accept things as they were, and if you didn't meet with him immediately, he was going to enforce that clause in your contract and you could kiss your money good-bye."

"He can't do that." She'd worked too hard for that money. Given up too much. Her time and her energy. Her heart.

"He wants to meet with you tomorrow," Darlene said.

"Impossible."

"But you said you'd be back tomorrow."

"I changed my mind. I was going to call you later and tell you. I haven't seen my mother in over six months. I figured another day wouldn't hurt." Now it seemed essential. She wasn't ready to face Cameron again.

"But you have to be here," Darlene insisted, a touch of alarm in her voice. "He was adamant about it."

"Tell him I'm in Wisconsin—" Peggi hesitated. "On business."

"I can't. I, ah—I already told him you were visiting your mother. He said he didn't care. You're to meet with him tomorrow morning at ten o'clock sharp."

"Ten o'clock? It's a five-hour drive from here back to Chicago. To make it by ten, I'll either have to leave this evening or very early tomorrow morning."

"Ten o'clock," Darlene repeated. "At his condo."

Darlene hung up the phone and faced Mitch. "Did I sound convincing?"

"Perfect."

"She almost messed us up. You're sure he'll be there?"

"I told him I'd meet him at ten. He wanted me to come by his office, but I convinced him that his condo was a better place to meet. I also talked to Pat and told her to call in sick tomorrow. That will leave them alone."

"Think it will work?" Darlene asked.

"With those two, who knows?"

At nine fifty-nine, Peggi stood in front of Cameron's door. She'd gotten the keys back from Darlene, but decided to knock. Hitting her knuckles against wood was actually satisfying. Three sharp raps could say a lot.

He took his time opening the door. Too much time, she decided, her anger increasing with each passing second. Who did he think he was, threatening to withhold her fee, making her drive back from her mother's? She'd done everything he'd wanted. His condominium was now a showplace of style and sophistication. She hadn't bothered him once since that morning when she'd stupidly blurted out that she loved him. She'd stayed away from his condo and hadn't called. There'd been no tears, no playing helpless, and no threats.

He was the one making threats.

The door opened, and he stood before her.

She would never get over the effect he had on her. A man shouldn't look so sexy. She shouldn't want what she couldn't have.

"Peggi?" He sounded surprised.

"Who did you expect? You said ten o'clock." She glanced at her watch. "It's exactly ten."

"I was expecting Mitch." He stepped into the hallway and looked toward the elevator.

"I haven't seen him." She needed space and headed for his living room. The sofa was why she was there.

Sitting on the Amritsar rug and next to the two blue

easy chairs, the cream-colored sofa looked great. Massive. Soft. Dramatic. Unless there was damage, she couldn't see his complaint.

She called back to him. "So what's wrong with it?"

"What do you mean, what's wrong with it?"

He'd closed the door and had come into the living room, but was standing back.

He was wearing a striped dress shirt, gray slacks, and black wingtips, but no tie or coat. His face looked tanner than she'd remembered, his eyes tired. Probably from the late hours he'd been keeping while in Bermuda. She didn't want to think of all the women he and his uncle had probably entertained while toasting their freedom. All she wanted to do was conclude this business and get on with her life.

Get him out of her life.

"What's so wrong with this sofa that you demanded I drive five hours from Wisconsin to meet you here this morning?"

"I didn't demand you drive anywhere." He glanced back at his door. "I was expecting Mitch at ten. He called yesterday and insisted we meet here this morning to go over some contracts."

"Mitch called you yesterday?" Peggi was beginning to understand. All too clearly. "I think we've been set up."

"Set up?" The lift of his eyebrows expressed Cameron's doubts.

"By Mitch and Darlene. She called me yesterday and said you'd demanded to see me at ten o'clock this morning—here. That you weren't happy with the sofa and were going to enact that clause in our contract if I didn't show."

"I never said that."

She was sure now that he hadn't. "They're playing games with us."

"Matchmaking?"

The word struck a chord, and she sucked in a breath. "So are you happy with the sofa?"

He glanced at it. "Yes. Of course. It's perfect."

"Good." She looked around, pleased with the way his entire condo had turned out. It would be a good advertisement for future business, in spite of the personal price she was paying. "In that case—"

She started to walk past him. He caught the sleeve of her coat. "Where are you going?"

Stopping, she faced him. "Back to the shop."

"To yell at Darlene?"

"Yes." No matter what Darlene's motives, there were no excuses for what she'd done.

"Pat called in sick this morning. At the time I thought she sounded funny. Now I understand."

"They wanted us alone?"

He nodded. "They've gone to a lot of trouble to get us together."

"Aren't friends great."

"Treasures." He didn't release his hold on her sleeve. His gaze caressed her face, and she felt her knees go weak. She searched for a level of sanity. "How was Bermuda? You didn't stay very long."

"I stayed long enough. It was an interesting experience."

"And have you now reaffirmed your affiliation in the confirmed bachelors' club?"

"My uncle's getting married."

Peggi laughed. It was too ironic. "There goes your ideal bachelor."

"It does hamper the image."

"I'm sure you tried to talk him out of it."

"I don't think I could have." He smiled. "You'll find this interesting. He got a phone call a few weeks ago. Almost a month after I'd talked to him. A call from a woman . . ." Cameron paused, his gaze going to his sound system. "A call he welcomed."

Peggi understood the significance of what he was saying. "Just like the psychic said would happen."

"Could be a coincidence."

"Could be." She didn't know what to think anymore.

"Do you remember I told you about a girl my uncle had dated all through high school? Clare?"

"I do. The one with the chronic backache that he always had to rub. Didn't she cry when he said he was going to work on a cruise ship, but he went anyway?"

"And was gone for five years. What I didn't know was when he came home, he'd planned on settling down and marrying Clare."

"Except . . . ?" She could imagine the rest.

"While he was away, Clare had gone and married someone else."

"Terribly inconsiderate of her."

"Irritated the hell out of him."

"You men." Peggi shook her head. "But now they're together?"

"Her husband died a few years back. Her youngest child is twenty. About a month ago she read about my uncle in a business magazine. The article stated that he lived part of the year in Bermuda, and she decided to track him down. Two days later she had his number and gave him a call."

"How do you feel about this?"

"About his getting married?" Cameron shrugged.

"It came as quite a surprise, to say the least. He'd never told me he'd planned on getting married. I've always thought of him as the carefree bachelor who could take a woman or leave her. I guess, from what he said this weekend, Clare marrying someone else really threw him for a loop. He couldn't talk about it, even to me, but he's always regretted leaving her."

"Strange," Peggi said.

"Actually, it's kind of wonderful." Cameron smiled. "You ought to see the two of them. They're like two lovebirds."

"Makes you wonder, doesn't it?"

"Wonder? Like, are we meant for each other? Was that psychic also right about us?"

There were times she'd hoped that was the case, but she gave him the answer she knew was more likely to be true. "Or wondered if what we've shared was simply lust?"

"You are one sexy lady." He smiled again. "Too bad you're also stubborn and outspoken."

"Oh, and you're not?" She lifted her chin. "You are probably the most stubborn man I have ever met."

"And irritating?"

"And irritating. Why I ever thought I was—" She nearly said the words, but stopped herself in time. His cocky grin said he knew what she'd been about to say.

He was irritating. No doubt about it. And it was time for her to make a hasty retreat before she really stuck her foot in her mouth.

She tried pulling her arm loose from his hold. She ended up being drawn closer, her body colliding with his and her hands grasping his arms for support. "Let me go!" she demanded.

He shook his head. "We were discussing why you thought you love me."

"I didn't say that." She'd come close, but close didn't count. "And if I had, it would have been 'loved,' past tense."

"You seem to fall in and out of love quite rapidly."

It wasn't true, but she didn't deny it. "A weakness of mine."

"Like falling for men who don't want to get married?"

"Maybe, deep down, I know I'm safe then."

"In other words, you don't want to get married."

His gravelly voice was too husky, his look too sensual. Keeping her composure at a distance was one thing. Staying composed when her coat was touching his shirtfront was another. "I didn't say that."

"Then what are you saying? That you want to get married?"

"No—yes." He had her completely confused. "I want to get married. Just not to you."

"Good." He smiled, but didn't loosen his hold. "Then we're agreed. Because, if I were to get married, I would want a wife who would enhance my career. Someone diplomatic."

"Definitely not me."

"Someone who wouldn't argue with my clients."

"Well, you've seen me in action there."

"George still mentions it."

"Good old George and Edna."

He chuckled. "If I were to marry you, I'd probably lose them as clients."

"I wouldn't want that to happen."

He looked down at her face, the green of his eyes as

rich as emeralds. "So now you agree with me? Success in business is more important than love."

"I didn't say that. What I meant was—" She stopped herself. Why argue over meaning? He hadn't changed his philosophy. "Cameron, let me go."

He released his hold and stepped back. She straightened the front of her coat, then ran her fingers through her hair. He never stopped watching her.

"I should be going," she said.

He nodded. "The job is finished. I'm more than satisfied, and the check will be in the mail, including the ten-percent bonus."

That surprised her. "I didn't finish before December first."

"You finished your part. It wasn't your fault I wanted an imported sofa and Christmas decorations."

"Well, thank you." She didn't move. This might be the last time she saw him. "And I'm glad you like what I did."

"I'll be doing more entertaining here now that the place looks respectable. Don't be surprised if you get some new clients after they see what you've done."

"I'm hoping I will."

There was really nothing more to say. She turned and started for the door. She was nearly to the foyer before he spoke her name. "Peggi?"

Heart in her throat, she turned and looked back. "Yes?"

"My uncle really seems happy, and the funny thing is, Clare's a lot like you."

"Really?"

"I wouldn't be an easy man to live with."

"No, you wouldn't be." Since that morning she'd

walked out on him, she'd told herself that over and over.

"I've lived by myself since—" He hesitated. "Well, for a long time."

Since Kara, she knew. She also knew what he was saying. "You're set in your ways."

"Definitely." He looked around. "Still . . ."

"What are you suggesting?" She was afraid to hope.

His gaze met hers again. "You were waiting for me, and that psychic said you were my soul mate."

"But . . . ?" She knew he had doubts.

"I don't know."

"I don't want to be considered a mistake."

He smiled and walked toward her. "You've been a mistake since the beginning. I never should have walked into your shop that first day."

"But you did." He'd stepped in looking like the playboy she'd read about only weeks before, and had turned her life upside down. "One thing I'm opposed to. I won't tolerate other women. I believe marriage should be a monogamous relationship."

"Already making the rules." He touched the side of her face, pushing her hair behind her ear.

He started to lean forward, and she knew he was going to kiss her. With a hand to his chest, she stopped him. "There's one thing more."

He straightened. "And what's that?"

She took in a shaky breath. "Do you love me?"

He hesitated. "I've missed you."

It wasn't enough. "If Darlene and Mitch hadn't set this up, would you have called me? Come after me?"

He didn't answer right away, and she knew the

truth. Closing her eyes, she gave up what she'd never had. "It won't work."

"He asked you to marry him, and you turned him down?" Darlene repeated, sinking onto the chair by Peggi's drafting table. "I don't believe you."

"He's not in love with me," Peggi answered, knowing what she'd done was for the best, no matter how much it hurt.

"He could learn to love you."

"He could also learn to despise me. You know yourself that marriage is risky enough. I'm not taking that kind of chance."

"Pat said he's been a bear since you stopped seeing him. Isn't that proof that he loves you?"

"I need the words, Dar. I need him to acknowledge what he feels is love."

Darlene shook her head. "You're throwing away a chance of a lifetime. He's good-looking, rich, and I have a feeling he's a hell of a lover."

Peggi could feel her cheeks growing warm. "Would you want a man who couldn't say he loved you?"

"He'll learn."

She doubted it.

Cameron stood at his window, watching soft, fluffy snowflakes drift downward. Below him, Chicago was dressed in her best, a cloak of darkness covering all signs of ugliness, while lines of headlights and flickering Christmas bulbs gave the illusion of joy. If the weathermen were right, by morning the city would be covered in a blanket of white.

From his living room came the soft New Age jazz strains of a Chris Speeris CD and behind him his computer monitor held the midweek assessment of the Dow Jones averages. He should feel good. Though the market was down, his clients were all showing gains, and the list he used in the Investment Club pool was making an equally good showing. No companies going bankrupt. He would be able to brag at his party Friday night. At this rate, he wouldn't be the loser hosting a get-together next year.

Wouldn't be trying to figure out the meaning of life.

He looked in the direction of Peggi's apartment. Was she home?

Was she as miserable as he was?

Somehow, somewhere along the way, he'd lost control. Three months ago he'd known where he'd been, where he was going, and how to get there. He'd had a plan, and his plan hadn't included a leggy, outspoken blonde.

Do you love me?

She'd asked him that question this morning, and he hadn't been able to answer. He still couldn't answer.

He wasn't even sure what love was.

If you love me, you won't go to Penn State, his mother had cried seventeen years ago, and he'd turned down the scholarship.

If you love me, you won't go to New York, Kara had yelled years after that.

Love confined.

Love hurt.

He was hurting.

Turning away from the window, he walked back to

his computer. He was in no mood to track highs and lows for the day. In no mood to study PE ratios.

He walked on.

In his refrigerator he found a bottle of imported beer. A twist and the cap was off, a soft fizz escaping. He sat on one of the stools at the breakfast counter and swallowed a gulp of the cold liquid, the slightly bitter taste not unlike the feeling he'd had all day.

Do you love me?

He knew he'd been out of sorts ever since he'd stepped out of his bathroom and found her gone. Nothing he'd tried in the last week and a half had chased away the feeling. It didn't help that he was surrounded by her, that everywhere he looked, he remembered something about her. Her indignation that day he'd pulled her onto the bed with him, the arguments they'd had over the rug in the living room. Her painting in his office was the essence of her—color, energy, and vitality.

He missed the vitality.

He should have stopped this before it ever got started, should have followed his instincts. He'd known she was trouble the first time they argued over his call to that radio station. Why hadn't he used a different decorator? It would have been so much safer.

Do you love me?

The words kept echoing in his head.

"I don't know!" he yelled into the empty room. "I don't know."

Setting the bottle down, he cradled his head in his hands.

She was driving him crazy.

❧————————❧

Peggi toweled herself dry after her shower, used the blower and a brush on her hair until it fell in silky waves around her shoulders, then she slipped on her flannel nightgown and slippers. The clock above her stove showed ten o'clock. Twelve hours earlier she'd been at Cameron's door. It seemed an eternity ago.

Do you love me? she'd asked him.

He'd never answered, which was her answer.

"Do you love him?" she asked herself, and sighed. That was the problem. She did.

She didn't want to. It wasn't in her best interest. Everything he'd said was right. She wasn't the type of woman a financial consultant should marry. She wasn't diplomatic enough. She never knew when to keep her mouth shut.

He wasn't the type of man she should marry. He had too many hang-ups. Why spend her life dealing with shadows from the past?

"Because he needs me," she said to her empty apartment. "And because I need him."

She didn't want to cry. The tears simply came, the sobs shaking her until she had to sit. All the anger and misery poured out, draining her physically as well as emotionally. She cried and she moaned, and she thumped the table with her fist.

She nearly didn't hear the other thump—the one on her door.

"Who's there?" she asked, wiping at her cheeks and eyes with the sleeve of her nightgown. She didn't think she'd been making so much noise that her neighbors would hear and complain, but perhaps she had been.

"Cameron."

His voice was unmistakable, the irritation in his

tone familiar. She didn't want to see him—not like this, not with her eyes red from crying. "Go away."

"Let me in."

"Go away," she repeated.

"I won't. Either you let me in, or I get the manager to let me in."

"He wouldn't do that."

"He will if I tell him you're suicidal."

That was all she would need. She stormed over to the door, released the locks, and jerked it open. "What do you want?"

He glanced down at her flannel nightgown and slippers, then up at her eyes. She knew how they must look. Even now they were watery. She wasn't going to apologize, however, or make excuses. "What do you want?" she asked again, her tone sharper.

He moved her aside and stepped into the room. "I want to talk."

The door across the hall opened a crack, and Peggi knew Mrs. Gilliatt was listening. She closed her door and faced Cameron. "We talked this morning. Remember?"

"You've been crying."

"So?"

He stepped toward her, his gaze again dropping to her nightgown. "What, no afghan?"

"I figured this covered me enough."

He grinned. "Nothing ever covers you enough."

She felt the butterflies in her stomach and tried to ignore them. The smell of beer was on his breath. "You've been drinking."

"Yes, but I'm not drunk, if that's what you're thinking. I'm stone-cold sober."

"Then why are you here?"

He smiled and touched her hair, lifting it away from her face with one finger to expose an ear, then letting it fall back into place. "Why am I here?" he repeated. "I am here to answer your question. The answer is yes."

"Yes?" She stared into his eyes, hoping she knew what he meant, but afraid to guess.

"Yes, I love you." He shook his head, looking none too happy about the confession. "That is, if love is being miserable the way things are, if love is needing to know I can see you again, that I can talk to you, argue with you—" He smiled. "Make love with you."

She didn't know what to say, the tears again forming in her eyes. Tears of happiness. She touched the lapel of his wool overcoat. "I'm sorry. I don't want to cry."

He brushed a fingertip under the base of each eye, wiping away the tears. "You have feelings," he said, and kissed her forehead. "You told me to expect this."

Straightening, he looked up at her ceiling. "You'll be pleased to know I also have feelings."

She wasn't sure she understood.

"I haven't cried in years," he said, still not looking at her. "Not since Kara. A defense, I suppose. I've built up a lot of defenses. You seem to be breaking them down."

She touched his cheek and felt the moisture. "Cameron?"

He looked at her and smiled, his eyes a liquidy green.

"I love you," she said.

He hugged her close, burying his face in her hair. "And I love you."

FOURTEEN

Darlene stood near one of her swag drapes, the window beside her looking out over Lake Michigan. It was cooler near the windows, less crowded. Cameron Slater's living room was filled to capacity with people, some elegantly dressed, others wearing the caterer's uniforms. In one corner a violinist and a cellist played Christmas songs. Earlier, the music had created a festive background. Conversations and laughter now nearly drowned out the sound.

All in all, Darlene had to admit, it was a great party. One she'd certainly never expected to attend. But then, these last few months had brought a lot of surprises.

She glanced toward the Christmas tree. Mitch looked dashing in a tuxedo. As far as she was concerned, he looked dashing in anything. She wasn't sure where they were headed, but she didn't care. He'd taught her to believe in herself, had restored her faith in men. Four more months and her divorce would be final, then she would think of the future.

Mitch smiled at her, then said something to the

man standing next to him and stepped away. He walked toward her, his gaze locked on her face, and she was certain no one could be as happy as she was.

Her gaze switched to the opposite side of the room. There might be one other person.

"I think Cameron's going to make the announcement soon," Mitch said, slipping an arm around her shoulders and looking the same direction.

"What do the people here think of her?" Darlene asked.

Mitch chuckled. "I don't believe the old guard knows quite what to think, especially considering what I heard her telling one of the wives. We're talking conservative Republicans here. She's as close to a flaming liberal as I can imagine, especially in that red dress. But Cameron can handle it."

"Peg's worried about him losing clients because of her."

Mitch shook his head. "What he loses, he'll gain other places. Tell her not to worry, she's exactly the balance he's needed. In spite of what the papers were printing, our Mr. Playboy was turning into a stodgy old grump. Now he's laughing. Enjoying life. He'll do fine and so will you guys. I'm hearing a lot of positive things about what you've done here. I think PDQ Interiors is going to be getting some calls after the first of the year."

"That's what we'd hoped."

"But, from what Cameron told me last night, you'd better leave the month of February open. That's when his uncle John is trying to book a church for the four of them."

"So what do you think?" Darlene asked. "Was that psychic right or what?"

"I'd say more right than 'what,' especially with a little help from us. Two more confirmed bachelors hit the dirt."

There was a clinking of metal against glass, and the conversations in the room began to subside. Cameron put the spoon down next to his glass and held up a hand, signaling the servers to stop moving among the guests and the violinist and cellist to stop playing.

When the room was quiet, he spoke.

"Ladies and gentlemen," he began. "As you know, you're here tonight because I'm a loser. However, I want you to know, I don't consider myself a loser. In fact, this week I became a winner. A big-time winner."

He slipped an arm possessively around Peggi's shoulders, drawing her to his side. "I would like to introduce my interior designer and my wife to be, Peggi Barnett."

Mitch smiled and whispered to Darlene, "I'm still glad she was the one waiting for him and not Pat."

THE EDITORS' CORNER

The four new LOVESWEPTs headed your way next month boast the sexiest season's greetings you'll ever read. While the chestnuts are roasting, be sure to treat yourself with romances guaranteed to put the sizzle in your holidays.

Marcia Evanick charms our socks off again with **MY TRUE LOVE GAVE TO ME,** LOVE-SWEPT #770. When she awakens Christmas morning, Megan Lemaine gazes, astonished, at the pear tree—with a partridge—in her backyard! Then Tate Brady comes courting, seducing her senses with fiery kisses while a dozen days of enchantment fill her with wonder. With this funny, touching, and utterly irresistible tale of love as magical as a Christmas miracle, Marcia Evanick creates a romance to cherish for always!

BORN TO BE WILD, LOVESWEPT #771, is

the next smoldering novel in Donna Kauffman's The Three Musketeers trilogy. Zach Brogan is sexier than sin, a globe-trotting wild man whose bad boy smile beckons Dana Colburne to taste thrills only he can deliver! He'd always sensed the secret wildness that burned inside his childhood pal, had tempted her into trouble more than once, but now he wants the woman she's become to feel his fire. Untamable, outrageous, explosively sexy, Donna Kauffman's heroes like dancing on the edge and women who don't make it easy— but no one sizzles hotter than guys who act bad to the bone but are oh-so-good!

Romantic Times award winner Laura Taylor explores the darkest shadows in the human heart with **SEDUCED**, LOVESWEPT #772. He'd loved Maggie Holden for as long as he could remember, had ached as she wed another, but now Noah Sutton wants to make the hauntingly beautiful widow his at last! Tainted by a tragic betrayal, her innocence destroyed, Maggie has retreated from the world. Noah stuns her with passion, igniting a soul-deep longing to be cherished—and to be believed. Rich with poignant emotion, thrilling in their intensity, Laura Taylor's novels celebrate the healing power of hope.

Bonnie Pega sets pulses pounding in **THE REBEL AND HIS BRIDE**, LOVESWEPT #773. Annabelle Pace was Gregory Talbot's true love, until she left him with no explanation. Now the beautiful seductress is back in town, and he is determined to get answers, if he can keep his hands off her delectable body long enough. Annabelle refuses to play second fiddle to the minister's causes, but with one kiss, he unleashes all her pent-up desires and recaptures her soul. Brimming with desire, Bonnie Pega offers a novel of passion too fierce to be denied.

Happy reading!

With warmest wishes,

Beth de Guzman

Shauna Summers

Beth de Guzman   Shauna Summers

Senior Editor   Associate Editor

P.S. Watch for these Bantam women's fiction titles coming in January: From Jane Feather—the incomparable author of the national bestsellers VIOLET and VALENTINE—comes **VANITY**, her newest unforgettable romance. **BREAKFAST IN BED**, a classic romance by *New York Times* bestselling author Sandra Brown, will be available in hardcover. In **DEATH ELIGIBLE** Judith Henry Wall sets out to discover how far one family will go to protect itself—when one of them is guilty of murder. Tamara Leigh, author of PAGAN BRIDE, presents **SAXON BRIDE**, the story of a fiercely handsome warrior and the breathtakingly lovely woman who leaves him torn between his duty and an agonizing truth. And finally, **NIGHT SINS**, the acclaimed national bestseller from Tami Hoag, will be out in paperback. Be sure to see next month's LOVESWEPTs for a preview of these remarkable novels. And immediately following this page, preview the Bantam women's fiction titles on sale *now*!

Don't miss these extraordinary books
by your favorite Bantam authors

On sale in November:

AMANDA
by Kay Hooper

HEAVEN'S PRICE
by Sandra Brown

MASTER
OF PARADISE
by Katherine O'Neal

TEXAS OUTLAW
by Adrienne deWolfe

When was the last time a novel seduced you?

With her spellbinding imagination and seductive voice, Kay Hooper is the only author worthy of being called today's successor to Victoria Holt. Now this powerful storyteller has created a unique and stunning tale of contemporary suspense that begins with a mysterious homecoming and ends in a shattering explosion of passion, greed, and murder. And all because a stranger says her name is . . .

AMANDA
by Kay Hooper

July, 1975

Thunder rolled and boomed, echoing the way it did when a storm came over the mountains on a hot night, and the wind-driven rain lashed the trees and furiously pelted the windowpanes of the big house. The nine-year-old girl shivered, her cotton nightgown soaked and clinging to her, and her slight body was stiff as she stood in the center of the dark bedroom.

"Mama—"

"Shhhh! Don't, baby, don't make any noise. Just stand there, very still, and wait for me."

They called her baby often, her mother, her father, because she'd been so difficult to conceive and was so cherished once they had her. So beloved. That was why they had named her Amanda, her father had explained, lifting her up to ride upon his broad shoulders, because she was so perfect and so worthy of their love.

She didn't feel perfect now. She felt cold and emptied out and dreadfully afraid. And the sound of her mother's voice, so thin and desperate, frightened Amanda even more. The bottom had fallen out of her world so suddenly that she was still numbly bewildered and broken, and her big gray eyes followed her mother with the piteous dread of one who had lost everything except a last fragile, unspeakably precious tie to what had been.

Whispering between rumbles of thunder, she asked, "Mama, where will we go?"

"Away, far away, baby." The only illumination in the bedroom was provided by angry nature as lightning split the stormy sky outside, and Christine Daulton used the flashes to guide her in stuffing clothes into an old canvas duffel bag. She dared not turn on any lights, and the need to hurry was so fierce it nearly strangled her.

She hadn't room for them, but she pushed her journals into the bag as well because she had to have *something* of this place to take with her, and something of her life with Brian. *Oh, dear God, Brian* . . . She raked a handful of jewelry from the box on the dresser, tasting blood because she was biting her bottom lip to keep herself from screaming. There was no time, no time, she had to get Amanda away from here.

"Wait here," she told her daughter.

"No! Mama, please—"

"Shhhh! All right, Amanda, come with me—but you have to be quiet." Moments later, down the hall in her daughter's room, Christine fumbled for more clothing and thrust it into the bulging bag. She helped the silent, trembling girl into dry clothing, faded jeans and a tee shirt. "Shoes?"

Amanda found a pair of dirty sneakers and shoved her feet into them. Her mother grasped her hand and led her from the room, both of them consciously tiptoeing. Then, at the head of the stairs, Amanda suddenly let out a moan of anguish and tried to pull her hand free. "Oh, I *can't*—"

"Shhhh," Christine warned urgently. "Amanda—"

Even whispering, Amanda's voice held a desperate intensity. "Mama, please, Mama, I have to get something—I can't leave it here, please, Mama—it'll only take a second—"

She had no idea what could be so precious to her daughter, but Christine wasn't about to drag her down the stairs in this state of wild agitation. The child was already in shock, a breath away from absolute hysteria. "All right, but hurry. And *be quiet.*"

As swift and silent as a shadow, Amanda darted back down the hallway and vanished into her bedroom. She reappeared less than a minute later, shoving something into the front pocket of her jeans. Christine didn't pause to find out what was so important that Amanda couldn't bear to leave it behind; she simply grabbed her daughter's free hand and continued down the stairs.

The grandfather clock on the landing whirred and bonged a moment before they reached it, announcing in sonorous tones that it was two A.M. The sound was too familiar to startle either of them, and they hurried on without pause. The front door was still open, as they'd left it, and Christine didn't bother to pull it shut behind them as they went through to the wide porch.

The wind had blown rain halfway over the porch to the door, and Amanda dimly heard her shoes squeak on the wet stone. Then she ducked her head against the rain and stuck close to her mother as they raced for the car parked several yards away. By the time she was sitting in the front seat watching her mother fumble with the keys, Amanda was soaked again and shivering, despite a temperature in the seventies.

The car's engine coughed to life, and its headlights stabbed through the darkness and sheeting rain to illuminate the graveled driveway. Amanda turned her head to the side as the car jolted toward the paved road, and she caught her breath when she saw a light bobbing far away between the house and the stables, as if someone was running with a flashlight. Running toward the car that, even then, turned onto the paved road and picked up speed as it left the house behind.

Quickly, Amanda turned her gaze forward again, rubbing her cold hands together, swallowing hard as sickness rose in her aching throat. "Mama? We can't come back, can we? We can't ever come back?"

The tears running down her ashen cheeks almost but not quite blinding her, Christine Daulton replied, "No, Amanda. We can't ever come back."

HEAVEN'S PRICE

by Sandra Brown

AVAILABLE IN PAPERBACK

"One of romance fiction's brightest stars."
—*Dallas Morning News*

With one huge bestseller after another, Sandra Brown has earned a place among America's most popular romance writers. Now the New York Times bestselling author of TEMPERATURES RISING brings us this classic, sensuous novel filled with her trademark blend of humor and passion, about a woman who thought she knew her destiny until she learns that fate—and her heart—have something else in store.

From the award-winning author of PRINCESS OF
THIEVES

MASTER OF PARADISE
by Katherine O'Neal

*As the privateer bore down on her ship, Gabrielle Ashton-
Cross recognized all too well the magnificent, leonine figure
at its prow. Once she had resisted his arrogant passion, had
survived his betrayal to become the toast of London. And
even now she might escape him, for her sword was like
lightning. Yet the moment their gazes locked across the
rolling deck, she knew that Rodrigo Soro had every intention of taming her to his will at last. Gabrielle hadn't
journeyed so far from home to fulfill a lifelong dream only
to surrender to a pirate king. But this time when he took
her in his arms, would she have the strength to fight the
only man who could ever promise her paradise?*

"Ella â minga," Rodrigo had told his men. *She's mine.*

He was so confident, so secure. Yet there were
some things even his carefully placed spies couldn't
know. Things that had long ago closed the door on
any future with Rodrigo—even if he hadn't thrown
his life away to become the bloodiest pirate of the
seven seas.

Gabrielle thought of that night, eight long years
ago, when they'd said their farewells. She'd seen the
proof back then of his dark passions, of the menacing

sensuality of the inner self he'd hidden from an unsuspecting world. Of the cold, ruthless way he could pursue his goals. Hadn't she learned that night to pursue her own aims just as coldly, just as ruthlessly? But she'd never seen this anger, this impression of raw, unrestricted violence that sparked the air between them. It scared her suddenly, as she realized for the first time where she was—alone in a locked room with the one man who was truly dangerous to her designs. With her ripped skirts up about her hips. With him pressing his all-too-persuasive body into the softly yielding flesh of her own. With an erection fueled by years of frustrated desires.

As if reading her thoughts, he softened his tone. Still holding her head in his hands, he said, "But that's over. We're together now. I've come here to rescue you."

She put her hands to his shoulders and pushed him away. "Just what is it you're rescuing me *from*?"

"From the clutches of England, of course."

She couldn't believe what she was hearing. "I rescued *myself* from England, thank you very much! Did you imagine I'd wait all this time, like some damsel in distress, for you to fashion a miracle and rescue me? When I had no indication that you ever thought about me at all?"

His hand stilled in the act of reaching for her breast. "I thought about you always. I never stopped longing for you."

"You never sent me word. Was I supposed to read your mind? Wait for a man who walked out of my life without so much as a backward glance? Without regrets of any kind?"

"You're wrong, Gabé. I regretted very much having to leave you behind."

"You *regret*? You knew what you were going to do and you didn't tell me. I can't believe the arrogance of you thinking you could waltz back into my life and dictate my future after all you did to me."

His hand made the arrested journey and slid over her breast. "Is a future with me so formidable a prospect?" he asked in a husky tone.

She shoved him away and fought to sit up. "Future? What kind of life would I have with you? A pirate's wench? Hunted by the law? Hung by the neck till I'm dead? You don't seem to understand, Rodrigo. You stand in the way of all I hold dear. You once told me I didn't fit into your plans. Well, now you don't fit into mine."

"You have no feelings for me at all, I suppose?"

She lifted her head defiantly and said, "None!"

He took her wrists and wrenched her up from the bed so she came crashing against his chest. The blow was like colliding with a brick wall. "I *know* you. I know the passions of your soul. It matters not what you say. You're mine now. This time I surrender you to no man. I made a mistake with you once before. But that," he added bitterly, "is a blunder I won't make again."

You're mine now. Staking his claim. Taking possession of her like a bauble he fancied. As if she had no feelings. Permitting her no say at all.

"I shan't let you do this," she vowed. "Your men already tried to take me against my will. Do you think I'd fight them off, only to let another pirate succeed where they failed?"

He was insulted, as she'd intended. She could see it in the tightening of his jaw, in the ferocious flare of his lion's eyes. She pulled away, but he followed, pushing her back to his bunk as he stepped toward her with stormy eyes. As she backed away across the expanse of red silk, she came up sharply against the wall—the one with the collection of weapons within handy reach.

He caught the flash of the blade as she snatched it from the wall. Incensed, he grabbed her arm and yanked her to her feet. But he didn't know what an expert swordswoman she'd become. Determined to fight him, she swung the sword around and put the cutting edge to his throat.

TEXAS OUTLAW

by Adrienne deWolfe

For a lady train robber, seduction was a game—until a handsome lawman changed the rules. . . .

In this sneak peek, Fancy Holleday has only a few minutes to dispose of Marshal Rawlins before her band of outlaws boards the train. And desperation drives her to a reckless act.

"Marshal!" Fancy's bellow rattled the windows and caused at least one passenger to douse his lap with turtle soup. "Arrest this man!"

"You want the preacher cuffed, eh?"

"Yes, sir, I most certainly do!"

"What in blazes for?"

Fancy hiked her chin. Obviously, Mama Rawlins had neglected to teach her son the finer points of etiquette.

"Because that . . . that *beast* of a man dared to . . ." She paused dramatically. "To grope me!"

Rawlins chuckled, a rich, warm sound in the breathless silence of the car. "Whoa, darlin'. No one was over there groping anything that you didn't give away a good long time ago."

She bristled. He had seen through her ruse! Despite her stylish emerald traveling suit and the demure black ringlets that framed her face, Cord

Rawlins had pegged her for a trollop. She wasn't sure she could ever forgive him for that.

"If you're not man enough to defend my honor," she said coolly, "then I shall be happy to speak to the railroad detective whom I saw dining here earlier."

Every eye in the car shifted eagerly back to Rawlins. He appeared undaunted. Hooking his thumbs over his gunbelt, he strolled to her side. She was surprised when she realized he was only about three inches taller than she. Standing in the doorway, he had appeared much larger. Nevertheless, the lawman exuded an aura of command.

"Well, preacher?" Rawlins tipped his Stetson back with a forefinger. A curl so dark brown that it verged on black tumbled across the untanned peak of his forehead. "Speak your piece."

The cleric continued to gape. "Well, I, um . . ."

"Spit it out, man. Did you or did you not grope this . . ." Rawlins paused, arching a brow at the straining buttons of Fancy's bodice. ". . . this, er, lady."

She glared into his dancing eyes, then let her gaze travel down his face. The man had dimples. Bottomless dimples. They looked like two sickle moons attached to the dazzling white of his grin. She thought there should be a law somewhere against virile Texicans with heart-stopping smiles. Cord Rawlins had probably left dozens of calf-eyed sweethearts sighing for him back home on the range.

"I'm sure there must be some reasonable explanation," the preacher meanwhile babbled. His scarecrow body trembled as he towered over Rawlins. "I'm sure the young lady just made a mistake—"

"The only mistake I made," Fancy interrupted, "was thinking that this lawman might come to the defense of a lady. No doubt Marshal Rawlins finds such courtesies an imposition on his authority."

"Begging your pardon, ma'am." He indulged her this time with a roguish wink. "I thought you did a mighty fine job of defending yourself."

Oh, did you now? She seethed. *Then just wait 'til you get a load of my .32!* If only that blessed moment would come. Where in hell was Diego?

"Show's over, folks." Rawlins waved his audience back to their meals. "Your pigeons are getting cold."

"That's it?" She gaped. "That's all you're going to do to help me?"

" 'Fraid so, ma'am. You aren't any the worse for wear, as far as I can see. And I reckon Parson Brown isn't any worse off, either."

"Why, you—!" Fancy remembered just in time that ladies didn't curse. "You can't just walk away," she insisted, grabbing Rawlins's sleeve and hoping he would mistake her panic for indignation.

"Says who?"

A nerve-rending screech suddenly pierced the expectancy in the car. Fancy had a heartbeat to identify the braking of iron wheels; in the next instant, the floorboards heaved, throwing her against Rawlins's chest. Silver, crystal, and a diner's toupee flew; she cringed to hear the other passengers scream as she clung to her savior's neck. Rawlins's curse ended in an "umph." Fancy was grateful when he sacrificed his own spine rather than let hers smash from the table to the carpet. For a moment, Rawlins's tobacco, leather, and muscled body imprinted themselves on her senses. Then her mind whirred back into action. She had to get his Colt.

Having made a career of outsmarting men, Fancy found it no great feat to shriek, thrash, and wail in a parody of feminine terror. She wriggled across Rawlins's hips and succeeded in hooking her heel behind his knee. She knew she could pin him for only a moment, but a moment was all she needed to slip her Smith & Wesson from her boot—and jam its muzzle into his groin.

"Whoa, darling," she taunted above the distant sounds of gunfire.

His face turned scarlet, and she knew he had assessed his situation. He couldn't reach his holster without first dumping her to the floor. And that would be risky, she gloated silently. Most risky indeed.

"Have you lost your goddamned mind?"

"My dear marshal, you really must learn to be more respectful of ladies," she retorted above the other passengers' groans. "Now real slowly, I want you to raise your hands and put them behind your head."

On sale in December:

BREAKFAST IN BED
by Sandra Brown

NIGHT SINS
by Tami Hoag
available in paperback

VANITY
by Jane Feather

DEATH ELIGIBLE
by Judith Henry Wall

SAXON BRIDE
by Tamara Leigh

OFFICIAL RULES ∾≈⊘≈∾ NO PURCHASE NECESSARY

To enter the sweepstakes outlined below, you must respond by the date specified and follow all entry instructions published elsewhere in this offer.

DREAM COME TRUE SWEEPSTAKES

Sweepstakes begins 9/1/94, ends 1/15/96. To qualify for the Early Bird Prize, entry must be received by the date specified elsewhere in this offer. Winners will be selected in random drawings on 2/29/96 by an independent judging organization whose decisions are final. Early Bird winner will be selected in a separate drawing from among all qualifying entries.

Odds of winning determined by total number of entries received. Distribution not to exceed 300 million.

Estimated maximum retail value of prizes: Grand (1) $25,000 (cash alternative $20,000); First (1) $2,000; Second (1) $750; Third (50) $75; Fourth (1,000) $50; Early Bird (1) $5,000. Total prize value: $86,500.

Automobile and travel trailer must be picked up at a local dealer; all other merchandise prizes will be shipped to winners. Awarding of any prize to a minor will require written permission of parent/guardian. If a trip prize is won by a minor, s/he must be accompanied by parent/legal guardian. Trip prizes subject to availability and must be completed within 12 months of date awarded. Blackout dates may apply. Early Bird trip is on a space available basis and does not include port charges, gratuities, optional shore excursions and onboard personal purchases. Prizes are not transferable or redeemable for cash except as specified. No substitution for prizes except as necessary due to unavailability. Travel trailer and/or automobile license and registration fees are winners' responsibility as are any other incidental expenses not specified herein.

Early Bird Prize may not be offered in some presentations of this sweepstakes. Grand through third prize winners will have the option of selecting any prize offered at level won. All prizes will be awarded. Drawing will be held at 204 Center Square Road, Bridgeport, NJ 08014. Winners need not be present. For winners list (available in June, 1996), send a self-addressed, stamped envelope by 1/15/96 to: Dream Come True Winners, P.O. Box 572, Gibbstown, NJ 08027.

THE FOLLOWING APPLIES TO THE SWEEPSTAKES ABOVE:

No purchase necessary. No photocopied or mechanically reproduced entries will be accepted. Not responsible for lost, late, misdirected, damaged, incomplete, illegible, or postage-die mail. Entries become the property of sponsors and will not be returned.

Winner(s) will be notified by mail. Winner(s) may be required to sign and return an affidavit of eligibility/release within 14 days of date on notification or an alternate may be selected. Except where prohibited by law, entry constitutes permission to use of winners' names, hometowns, and likenesses for publicity without additional compensation. Void where prohibited or restricted. All federal, state, provincial, and local laws and regulations apply.

All prize values are in U.S. currency. Presentation of prizes may vary; values at a given prize level will be approximately the same. All taxes are winners' responsibility.

Canadian residents, in order to win, must first correctly answer a time-limited skill testing question administered by mail. Any litigation regarding the conduct and awarding of a prize in this publicity contest by a resident of the province of Quebec may be submitted to the Regie des loteries et courses du Quebec.

Sweepstakes is open to legal residents of the U.S., Canada, and Europe (in those areas where made available) who have received this offer.

Sweepstakes in sponsored by Ventura Associates, 1211 Avenue of the Americas, New York, NY 10036 and presented by independent businesses. Employees of these, their advertising agencies and promotional companies involved in this promotion, and their immediate families, agents, successors, and assignees shall be ineligible to participate in the promotion and shall not be eligible for any prizes covered herein. SWP 3/95